Please feel free to send me an
filters these emails. Good new

Desirae Clark- desirae_clark@awesomeauthors.org

Sign up for my blog for updates and freebies!
desirae-clark.awesomeauthors.org

About the Publisher

BLVNP Incorporated, A Nevada Corporation, 340 S. Lemon #6200, Walnut CA 91789, info@blvnp.com / legal@blvnp.com

Praise for MY BAD BOY NEIGHBOR

I thought it was fantastic. Probably one of my favorite books I have ever read. I majorly recommend it. [The] ending was [so] unsuspected, but so is life, so it was appropriate. [It's] not 100% what you think when you hear the title. [There] are many life lessons inside this wonderfully-written book.— Eryn, *Goodreads*

I highly recommend this book to all of you. The book is worth a read. It's a cute story about a beautiful, smart girl [crossing] paths with a handsome bad boy[.] As simple as it seems, it is a [fun-filled] adventure.— Risha, *Goodreads*

This book is incredibly witty and has the most relatable main character I've encountered in a while. [The] story is mostly light, but it also touches a couple of dark subjects (grief, anxiety, etc.). I loved the ending and am really looking forward to reading the sequel.— Anya Blackhart-Clark, *Goodreads*

MY BAD BOY NEIGHBOR

Desirae Clark

BLVNP

ISBN: 978-1-68030-815-0

Table of Contents

To Anya, Sale, Kristina, and my dad. You have always been there for me and kept me from giving up.

To Sasha Alsberg, whose passion for books infected me as well. If she didn't reply to me and encouraged me to start writing, this book wouldn't even exist.

To my friends, my family, and my readers. Sometimes in our lives, we find ourselves dreaming and hoping. May your dreams and hopes come true just like mine did. Thank you for your unlimited, unconditional love and support.

Free Download

Get these freebies and *more* when you sign up for the author's mailing list!

desirae-clark.awesomeauthors.org

Chapter 1

Dear Diary,

You know who I am, Astrid Ella Bailey, my school's loser nerd, my brother's annoying sister, the daughter my parents never find time for, and now that things finally got so bad, I decided to write to you. It feels weird, though. It's as if I am talking to myself. Then again, I always find writing, as well as reading, my escape.

I am still trying to cope with the way things are for me, and I just need to voice my opinions. I feel stuck, and though I have friends, I can't come to them with anything. So here I am, writing about everything that's going on in my life.

I have two years of high school left, and in the future when I look back, I want them to be remembered. Maybe I'll even read this diary to my future kids when they're old enough and shake my head at all the bad decisions I have made. Maybe I'll look back and think about everything I went through and how I made it to where I'll be at that point in the future.

But let's not get sidetracked. I want to start by telling you about today. It was supposed to be a day just like any other. I had plans to get out of my more than comfortable bed like I usually did and complete my morning routine I had set for myself a long time ago. Instead, it went in a quite unusual direction.

I woke up thirty minutes late, and that alone sent me into panic mode right away. I was a perfect student who never skipped classes and made sure my grades were more than flawless. Hurriedly, I got up to take my everyday morning shower and, unfortunately, realized my idiotic twin brother had used all the hot water. To make matters even worse, I bumped my pinkie toe into a table and almost tripped over my 'I Read YA' doormat in front of my bedroom. (I got it when I went to a reader's convention in Chicago last year.)

Because the cold water made my hair frizzy, it got hard to brush through, and that introduced me to a brand-new problem—barely getting ready in time. Being late was never an option for me. I was either at school, or I was on my deathbed. There was no in-between.

I went downstairs to the kitchen to make myself some breakfast when I looked at the clock. I didn't have enough time to eat without being late. So I simply took an apple, and before I knew it, it was seven AM, and I was rushing to my car. My bag landed on the back seat where I threw it before I heard my brother call after me.

"Astrid, wait!" Connor rushed through the front door, trying to catch his breath. His dark brown hair was a mess, and I guess he slept in too. That meant he now wanted to ask me for a ride. It's a rare thing, but I witness it every now and then.

My brother and I are two very different people. While I would describe myself as a socially awkward seventeen-year-old with a serious addiction to books and anything book related, my brother is the social butterfly of my high school. He is the captain of Evergreen High's football team, the star athlete, and one of the most popular guys in school.

We are twins, but while he is extremely talkative (and annoying), I keep quiet most of the time. My brother likes to slack off, taking the term *couch potato* to a whole new level, and I like to be kept busy. In short, he is highly—and I mean it—disorganized and popular while I am not.

"What do you want now?" I asked with disinterest and walked over to the driver's side.

"I need a ride," Connor said to me.

"Call your friends," I told him, trying to wave him off as I opened the driver's door. He simply ran a hand through his annoyingly good-looking hair as if he was bragging about getting all the good genes in this family.

"They already left. Now get in the car and drive. Otherwise, we're going to be late, and you know I can't miss my morning practice," Connor ordered before he slid into the passenger seat without waiting for an answer.

I knew that Coach had been pushing them extra hard this year for some unknown reason. I hate American football, though. I always have and always will. That's mostly because my brother keeps boasting to people about how good he is at it and use girls with its help, *and* also because I suck at it.

I am sure other girls could and should play American football if they wanted. It was just my choice to stay away for the greater good.

I rolled my eyes, told him to fasten his seat belt, and started the car. We spent most of the drive in silence, him texting someone and me being focused on the road. Then *it* happened.

Faster than anything in this world, someone's car crashed into mine and sent us sliding across the street where we finally came to a stop. I didn't even hear the crash, but I felt its impact because it threw Connor and me both forward, the seat belts cutting into our chests and forcing our breaths to leave our bodies.

This was my first car accident ever, and I didn't know how to react. I was not able to comprehend what just happened and couldn't get myself together.

My brother and I both struggled to unfasten our seat belts. There was smoke coming from the front of our cars, and I had to cough a few times before I could finally breathe again. I opened my car door and almost collapsed. If it was because of shock or the collision, I had no idea.

I checked for any sign of injuries, but nothing was seriously hurt. Suddenly, I heard another car door open and close, but it was not Connor's. My neck ached when I looked up to the driver.

The driver was none other than Kai Asher, the school's Bad Boy (with capital Bs) and one of the most attractive guys. Getting noticed by him meant getting instant bad reputation and days—if he stuck around that long—of starring in school gossips.

His dark hair and brown eyes were swoon-worthy. Maybe it was the way he smiled, showing his pearly white teeth, or the fact that he had been in detention more times than I could count, but something was definitely clear about him. He could be on the school's football team, and he could be one of my brother's buddies, *but* he was definitely trouble.

"Are you crazy? How fast were you driving?"

I didn't know whether it was from shock, but I never would've yelled at anyone like that. My insides were shaking, and I was surprised by the swirling emotions I felt inside—confusion, anger, fear, shock.

"Excuse me, princess, but you came out of nowhere." He ignored my question, running a hand through his dark hair. His voice remained calm like nothing in the world could disturb him. Not even an accident and with our cars most likely wrecked beyond repair.

"I was driving by the speed limit! How can you blame me for this?" I said incredulously. His calm manner fuelled my rage and all my emotions. Just because he was popular and good-looking, didn't mean he always got everything he wanted. The girls caved in, the guys followed his command, and to top it all off, he was annoyingly arrogant. His ego was over the roof, but I mattered too. My opinion mattered, or so I wanted to think.

"My car is ruined. Oh God, I'm going to be in so much trouble," I said after a few moments of silence as the situation started to sink in. To keep my hands from shaking, I wrapped them around my body.

"Oh, please, you're such a typical good girl. All you worry about is not getting into trouble, getting high grades, and keeping your parents happy." Kai snapped as if he actually knew me. He was right, though, and for the first time, I felt a little ashamed to admit it. I wasn't ashamed of being a good girl. I was ashamed to admit he was right. He did know me—well, kind of.

Looking at Kai Asher—the one classmate I wasn't particularly fond of, especially at this moment—he seemed a bit angry, but if you looked twice, you noticed he was actually amused. I wanted to smack him so badly, and his comment irritated me more than I would care to admit.

"So, what do we do?" I asked because one, he seemed to have all the answers and two, I suddenly felt too tired to argue.

A thought came to me then, and I felt horrible for not thinking about him before. My brother. I turned around immediately and barely noticed he was talking over the phone a couple of meters back. He hastily finished his conversation and then turned to me.

"I see you two are done bickering. I called our parents and the police. They'll be here any moment now, and we're all excused from classes. And good to see you, dude," my brother said, making me frown.

Good to see you?

My parents forbade me from driving my car—mostly because it wasn't anywhere near driving condition. I felt sad since that was my first car and it held so many memories of me along with my two best friends, road trips, and my weekly trips to the Winterheart bookstore.

Winterheart was our local bookstore that had way more books than you could wish for. Going there topped meeting your favourite celebrity or bumping into your favourite booktuber on a mission to film a book haul. It topped all the Christmas presents you got as a kid.

To get back to the point, my car was the most reliable source of transportation I had, and now it was gone.

When we got home, the first thing I did was check my cell phone. I noticed several missed calls and texts from my best friend Addie. Instead of calling her back, I texted her a short explanation as to why I was a no-show at school, but I was also smart enough to leave out the part mentioning Kai Asher as the driver at fault.

Later, I just sat down and read the last ten pages of a book I started reading yesterday. I didn't realize how exhausted I truly was until my eyes started to close and sleep took over.

It was dark when I woke up, and I heard loud music playing. At first, I thought it was Connor, and I wanted to yell at him, blurt out a few threats, and then go back to sleep, but as I entered the hallway, I realized the sound wasn't coming from that direction. It wasn't coming from my house at all.

Oh no. I followed the sound only to lead me to my window where I could see the house next door. To make things even weirder, it had its light on for the first time in *years*. It had been empty for a long time.

After a few moments of collecting myself, I drew the curtains to the side and opened my window. The sight in front of me was so shocking, and I was already at the point where I felt like nothing could surprise me by now.

Never in a million years would I have expected to see *him*—twice in one day—singing shirtless and doing some crazy dance moves while every muscle stood out in his very, very defined body. Kai Asher's dark hair was messy, which made his bad boy attitude totally work. If today hadn't happened, then maybe I would even swoon over him, but I didn't.

Instead, I was staring like an idiot until I got to my senses—which took longer than I cared to admit—and cleared my throat. He turned around abruptly, his mouth forming a perfect smile.

If it was my turn to smirk as if I caught him doing something embarrassing, then I wouldn't have realized it. He seemed proud of it, and teasing him about this...*scene* wasn't an option.

"Hey, princess. I see you just can't stay away from me, can you?" He winked, which he did a lot. What a flirt! And what was worse was that girls fell for his charms. Maybe I would've too if his attitude didn't bother me so much.

Call me a drama queen. I don't care. He should take responsibility for his actions and at least apologize. I think that would be better than nothing.

I tried not to roll my eyes, partly because I had trouble peeling them off his body, and partly because I needed to be nice. If

I wasn't, this could seriously backfire in my face. So, I put my sweet face on and talked to him as nicely as I could. "Listen, can you keep it down? Some people are actually trying to do something productive like read, sleep, or maybe even study," I said, and the response I got was his amusement.

"And singing isn't productive? Don't deny that you like staring at me without a shirt on." Kai teased me, and I actually snorted when he gestured to his body.

"I do not! And I woke up thanks to your music." I defended myself, but it was hopeless. I could feel the heat spreading through my cheeks while I forced myself to look at his eyes.

"Ah, so that explains the way you look," he said to me, leaning his arms on his window and mimicking my position. We were a couple of feet apart, which didn't seem far enough.

"Excuse me?" I asked him, almost unable to comprehend his words. There was a tree between us so that one could easily climb over. Our houses were built really close just like every house in the neighbourhood.

"Your hair is so messy. I thought you were going to a carnival," Kai explained. I felt embarrassed, but I would not admit it. I may be a good girl, and that might be a blow—a popular guy from school saying you look horrible—but I knew when to keep my mouth shut for the sake of keeping my sanity.

Instead, I picked up the closest thing to me, which happened to be a pencil, and threw it at him. Needless to say, I missed. Damn you, sports! Why can't I be good at anything? Ugh.

And damn it! I just realized that it was my good luck pencil, the one I did my math homework with. But being too proud to ask for it back, I opted for the better option—insulting him.

"You're an ass," I told him. "Why are you even staying at that house?"

"I just moved here," Kai explained with even more humour in his voice as if this amused him to no end. I froze, and my face must have been freaking hilarious because he couldn't keep himself from laughing. "Looks like we're going to be neighbours, princess." He gestured to the boxes in his room.

"Oh God." I groaned. I'd have to actually use my curtains from now on. "Just keep the damn music down," I said and closed my window. I heard him laugh, but he did as I asked.

Chapter 2

Morning couldn't have come any sooner. I felt that I'd barely even closed my eyes and the alarm clock rang. It was five o'clock sharp when I got up from my bed with a bang.

Literally.

I rolled over the edge of my bed and hit my head against the floor. What was with me and clumsiness these last few days? I was never clumsy. I got up with a grunt and took a steaming hot shower that woke me up a bit more. I was satisfied that today was not as disastrous as the day before. I put on some makeup afterwards because I liked wearing it. It made me feel more comfortable, and I hated it when people suddenly thought that just because I was smart and a so-called nerd, I would skip out on it.

I put on some clothes and continued with my morning ritual. We didn't have any exams yet—thank God—but I still liked to be prepared. When I went through all my notes, I decided to switch and start reading. With a book in hand, I headed downstairs to make myself some breakfast.

Halfway through my meal, I heard a loud *thump, thump, thump* noise nearing me. This could only mean one thing. My brother's footsteps got even more thunderous when he arrived at the kitchen. He barely bothered to glance my way, but he did say hi, which was a record on the Connor scale.

"My friends are picking me up, so I'm going. Don't forget to lock after you leave. Mom and Dad probably won't be home today," he informed me. Connor could drive himself, but my parents refused to buy him a car because he was a terrible and absolutely horrible driver. His driving was worse than catastrophic or disastrous. I still wondered how he got his license in the first place, but what Connor wanted, he got.

"Oh, I forgot to ask my friends if they could give me a ride," I said partly to myself. I felt stupid for not thinking about it. Just when I thought nothing could go wrong today, I found out I spoke too soon.

"Good luck getting to school on time. Matt's car is already full." Connor smirked at me, and I wanted to throw something to wipe it off his annoying face. He enjoyed this *a lot* because he was always a jerk. He liked to see me struggle in life like it brought him some kind of happiness.

Connor and I both heard a car coming and slowing down in front of our house, so he didn't even bother saying goodbye to me— at least out of politeness. The only thing he did was turn and leave. As soon as he got in Matt's car, they sped down the street with the music blasting louder than it should be legal.

There once was a time I liked Matt, which was one of those parts of my life I never talked about. Mostly because he was always a total asshat to me. Just like my brother, Matt often found ways to torment me by calling me stuff or acting like I was a waste of space. He often called me ugly, lame, useless, and every other hurtful thing he could think of. Most of the time, I was referred to as the loser of my family. The sad thing was I often took comfort in the fact he never called me stupid. It's the one thing he couldn't take away from me. At that time, my self-esteem was at its lowest, and to make matters even worse, I was going through a rough patch in my life. Then again, one could never expect Matt Jackson and my brother to be considerate. I was used to being in everybody's way by now, so I plainly resigned myself to solitude.

I found my phone and walked out the door where I sat on the stairs. The sun was already high up in the sky as I dialled one of my best friends' number. Diana lived twenty minutes away and picked up her phone pretty soon.

"Astrid! Where are you? Addie and I've been worried sick."

If they'd been so worried, why didn't I get a single text?

"Um...I'm at home. I kind of got stood up by my brother, and I need a ride to school. Can you come pick me up?" There was an awkward silence after that, and I just wanted to die.

"Oh, As, I'm sorry, but we have classes in fifteen minutes. It takes us ten minutes to get to your house, and even with Addie's mega fast driving, we wouldn't make it back in time. You know how uptight our parents have been these last few weeks about skipping school."

"Yeah, I know. I get it. I'll think of something," I said and hung up on her.

I did it mostly because I didn't want to fight. She and Addie have been skipping school all the time, but when I needed them, they blew me off. I wanted to scream, but instead, I just let out a loud, frustrated sigh. Putting my head on my hands, I thought about all my other options. There was the bus, but it wouldn't come for twenty more minutes. I guess I could just cycle. However, I wouldn't be there in time, anyway. I might as well have walked and made a quick stop at Starbucks.

"Having a bad day?" I heard a deep voice say, snapping me out of my thoughts. All I could think was *'Oh, not him. Not now. Just go away.'*

When I looked up and saw a smirking Kai standing before me, I immediately averted my gaze to the ground.

"Why do you care?" I muttered, clenching my teeth.

"What's wrong?" He ignored my question as he sat down next to me on the stairs in front of my house. I met his gaze, thinking that this dude was an expert when it came to timing. His smirk was gone, only to be replaced by a hint of worry. *Like he actually cared*, a malicious voice inside my head said, and I knew it wasn't so far from the truth.

"Nothing. It doesn't matter," I said and bit my lip.

"That's bullshit," he blurted out.

"What are you doing here, anyway? Shouldn't you be in school being entertained by a flock of Barbies?" I snapped because he wouldn't leave me alone. I didn't want him here, nor did I want to discuss my day with someone who practically caused all this. Also, I hated that I sounded like I was his jealous girlfriend.

"I'm planning on going. Still have five more minutes."

"Oh, right, I forgot. Fast driver." I rolled my eyes, remembering how fast his car hit mine yesterday. Then the consequences of that and what could have happened came rushing to my mind. He nodded before his shoulder playfully hit mine.

"What about you, princess? Shouldn't you be in school?" he asked with a smile, daring me to play his game, and I didn't know how he did it, but his playful attitude immediately got me in a better mood.

"Yes, but you destroyed my car, remember?" I replied shortly, sighing. "Poor Jinx."

"You named your car Jinx?" Kai chuckled. "You practically jinxed it."

"Shut up. Yes, I named my car Jinx. So what? Stop laughing at me," I muttered, but really, I felt embarrassed. I felt uncomfortable around him and wished, if only for a brief moment, that I could disappear.

"You look adorable when you blush," Kai said to me before he got up and offered me his hand. I gave him a puzzled look to which he only replied with, "Come on, sweetheart. I owe you a ride."

Chapter 3

He brought me over to his driveway, the driveway of a house I'd never been to yet seen more often than I could count. Kai stopped in front of his motorcycle and turned to me smirking.

"I'm afraid of going on this thing," I said in all honesty and stepped back, clearly intimidated.

"Come on." Kai sighed, grabbing my hand. I tried to move it away, but it was too late. His hand was warm and inviting, but I couldn't do it.

"I don't think it's safe for anyone to ride this *thing*," I said in protest as he made me step closer to his motorcycle. I always hated motorcycles because it looked very easy to die on them. They might have looked cool, but logic told me it didn't take much to kill you, especially when speed was involved.

"Scared?" Kai teased, turning around. It was clear he tried not to smile, but a chuckle still left his lips. Just because he offered to help me, didn't mean that I liked the guy. I still couldn't stand him and his big ego.

He let go of my hand, and I wrapped my hands around my body. That was my way of protecting myself though there might not be any real danger there.

"I'm not exactly...scared. You're just not that protected like you are in a car." I blushed, feeling embarrassed and weird. "And anyway, I'm still a little shaken up from yesterday's events, and you can't really expect me to be fine with riding on a motorcycle handled by a dude I barely know just because he goes to the same school." I tried to argue.

"And also because he's your new neighbour," Kai added, clearly not wanting to let this go. He handed me his helmet, put on his own, and climbed on the bike. When I hesitated, he looked at me. "We're kind of on a tight schedule, princess. You coming or not?"

"I guess I don't have any other choice." I sighed in defeat. I got on reluctantly, hoping I would stay alive. I wrapped my arms around him, and a sense of unfamiliarity washed through me. The way his muscles felt against my arms, or how warm he was in this somewhat cold weather unnerved me.

It was the first time I was this close to a guy, and it felt strange. Kai's hands brushed mine for a second before he said, "Hold on tight, sweetheart." And then we took off. I think he enjoyed watching me squirm almost as much as Connor did. He was, after all, on the same team as my brother.

The minute he drove out of his driveway and onto the road, I expected him to drive a lot faster, but he didn't. Maybe he was slowing down because of me.

Oh, who are you kidding, Astrid? He's not slowing down because of some girl. He's Kai Asher for love's sake, my inner voice broke my chorus of thoughts.

We took a left turn and drove through some more streets when we got stopped by a traffic light. I looked around me and noticed our school was only two minutes away.

The moment the traffic light turned green, we sped through the streets and turned into the school's parking lot. A lot of people were there, and a lot of people were expecting Kai. What they weren't expecting was *me*.

He parked his motorcycle in an empty spot near an entrance, so I let go of him to climb off the bike. He followed, and I handed him the helmet he gave to me. People were staring at us, probably thinking the school's loser was sleeping with the bad boy and trying to get higher on the popularity scale.

"Thanks for the ride," I said to him with restraint, trying to be nice, but I knew there was something ungrateful in my voice. As happy as I was to be in school, I knew the consequences of appearing with him. I turned to leave when I heard him speak.

"No problem, princess."

I smiled slightly and shook my head at his weird thing for nicknames. As I made my way to the front door of my school, I tried to get away from the people who kept staring at me—cheerleaders, jocks, other nerds, and almost everybody who could see. Kai drew a lot of attention, and now I was a part of it. I dreaded the rumours that were bound to follow.

I kept my head low and hurried to my locker, avoiding people's gazes and the hostile looks I got from some girls. I hated it. I hated the attention. By the time I got there, the bell had ringed, and students went into their different classrooms. I had an art class as my first period, and I shared it with my best friend Diana. It was a really boring class, but I loved it because Diana and I had the opportunity to chat. I often tended to zone out, though.

"Astrid, are you even listening to me?" Diana asked as I was sketching into my poor, wrecked art notebook.

"Kind of," I told her. "Something about a shopping mall and some cute red shoes," I repeated what I remembered from the story she'd been telling me for the past fifteen minutes. The only reason why I tuned out was because Diana had a tendency to drift away from the point and talk about other irrelevant stuff.

"Yes. I saw these really, really cute red shoes yesterday when Addie and I went shopping after school, but I didn't have enough money because my stupid mom had problems with her bank and couldn't give me my monthly allowance. Anyway, not to get off topic—I was there with Addie, and we saw these cute shoes, but me having no money is not the worst part. Do you know what the worst part is? No, of course, you—"

"Just tell me what the worst part is!" I said in annoyance because she always kept rambling. I was also annoyed with her because she and Addie went to the mall without even asking me—I would have said no, but it would feel nice to be invited anyway—and because she talked of her mom that way. Her mom was the sweetest person ever, and at least, Diana's mom was home every day, unlike my parents who worked all the freaking time.

"The worst part is that Matt's girlfriend, you know—Cindy or whatever her name is—got the last pair of those shoes, and I'll never see them again." Diana got really angry because she disliked Cindy. No, *disliked* doesn't cover it. We all *hated* her personality. Not only was she as bad as Matt, she was way worse. If something didn't go her way, she would throw a tantrum like a kid. She was spoiled, ungrateful, and viciously mean.

"That's sad," I said to Diana with not much emotion. I liked clothes and shoes, but I wasn't as obsessed as her. She needed all the brands and everything that was in style.

My two best friends were popular and loved while I was fairly ignored and disliked. It was a miracle we stayed friends through all these years considering how different we were.

Diana wrapped her arms around my waist and pretended to grieve after that gorgeous pair of shoes. I patted her back and then let her go. "Think about it this way—they wouldn't go with your cheerleading outfit anyway," I said, and I knew it was the only thing that would make her feel better.

Diana smiled sadly, and we talked some more, laughed, and did anything but mention about this morning until the bell rang and we both went our separate ways.

Chapter 4

Diana and I went to meet Addie, who had been waiting for the sole reason that we shared the same locker. While we were walking through the halls, passing people who were giving me shocked and outraged looks, Addie decided to strike up a conversation.

"So, guess what I heard from *Mattie*," Addie said loud enough for only Di and me to hear. Diana was now looking around, confused by the looks and the whispers people were giving me. I tried to keep my head down and stay unnoticed, but it was impossible because I was surrounded by my two best friends. They were attention magnets.

"Apparently, our good little girl caught a ride with the school's bad boy today. On a motorcycle too."

The good girl here was me, obviously. "Wait." Diana whipped around, her blonde hair falling over her shoulders as her blue eyes bore into mine. "Which one of the school's BBs? Hunter Riley?"

Adelaide shook her head and replied, mesmerized, "Kai Asher himself."

Both of my friends floated away to their own universes as they thought about Kai, or so I assumed. Kai was quite respected around here, the star of the school, if you didn't count my brother. He was desired by everyone though he never had anything with my best friends. Mostly because they considered themselves out of his league—actually, everybody else in this school considered him out of theirs.

I knew I was so busted that they found out about what I did this morning with Kai. A wave of gratitude spread through me when we reached our locker. I felt my cheeks heat up, but thankfully, the girls didn't notice because the locker door hid me. It goes without saying that I basically stuffed my face inside it. I put in all our books and took out the other ones we were going to need.

"Is this true?" Diana said half-heartedly, and I nodded. I knew she was picturing Kai's abs, his warm yet dark brown eyes, and that amazing, perfect smile. And somehow, I was caught imagining it myself. As soon as I realized what I was doing, I cleared my throat, shook my head, and closed my locker.

"Okay, we're clearly missing something here. Spill," Addie demanded with a smile. Out of the three, she was definitely the calm one. She ran a hand through her brown hair and prepared herself for my answer.

"There's nothing to spill. You guys didn't want to pick me up, and I clearly said that I was going to figure something out. He just happened to be around," I confessed. It was true, but I *"accidentally"* happened to miss out a couple of very important details.

What they don't know can't hurt them, right? I thought.

"Uh-huh. Bullshit. Tell us what happened and how the hell does Matt know about this?" Diana said to me first, but then she turned to Adelaide.

"Beats me. All I know is what I heard although I could tell he wasn't exactly happy." Addie knew everything that happened in this school. It was like walls had ears, and they were hers. She was super popular, and so was Di, but only because they knew so many people and they were both gorgeous.

"He probably saw Kai and me when we pulled into the school's parking lot. Everybody there was staring." I tucked a strand of hair behind my ear. I knew that my brother found out by now and was going to kill me. He acted like a jerk, but he also didn't want me hanging out with anyone other than girls. He tended to be overprotective, but it was just a way to isolate me from the crowd. Which I had to admit, I didn't mind at all.

"Oh, your brother's going to freak out." Diana practically read my thoughts. "And since Matt isn't exactly the happiest I've seen him today, I would suggest you hide."

"Let's just go to class. I don't want to be late," I said quietly, trying to change the subject. Walking towards the English classroom I shared with both my best friends, I sat down just as the bell rang. Di and Addie sat together, and the seat beside me was empty.

I was getting ready, trying to avoid people's stares and minding my own business because I felt absolutely uncomfortable. Then something shocking happened—someone sat down next to me. At first, I didn't look up because I was busy putting my books on my desk, but when I did, I saw a pair of brown eyes smiling at me. They belonged to the one and only Kai. The Bad Boy in capital letters.

I suddenly gulped, intimidated by him. He seemed nice to me, but there was definitely something he wanted. Never before had anyone like him acknowledged the existence of someone like me. Not at school—not in front of everybody.

Kai never sat down next to anyone. It was worrying that he chose his seat right next to me, and everybody else seemed to be taken aback by it as well. There was a short silence in the classroom before the whispers started. I felt my throat closing up. I felt anxious for him to leave.

Reminding myself how to breathe, I mustered up all the courage to steal a look at him.

"Hey, princess," he said to me once he got comfortable in his seat. I immediately looked down at my book.

"What are you doing here?" I whispered, desperate not to attract any more attention from our classmates, but I knew it was hopeless. Everybody was staring. The only good thing was that nobody was staring at me but at Mr. Sex on Legs beside me.

Crap. Did I really just think that?

I really was a hopeless case, wasn't I? I was such a Good Girl (with capital Gs) that even thinking those kinds of thoughts made me feel dirty, really dirty.

"Where?" He played dumb. "The universe, Earth, America, this city, classroom…" Kai was smirking now, but it wasn't anything compared to the way his brown eyes shone as he gazed into mine. It was not hard to know he was trying to have a go at me.

"Here, as in sitting next to me." I tried to be more specific, but it was clear in my tone he annoyed me a little.

"Well, it's a free country. Unless this is your boyfriend's seat."

"Oh, shut up," I ordered, and he did even though he was amused, and I could tell he enjoyed getting on my nerves. I kept stealing glances on my sketchbook, unsure if I should continue doing what I usually did in English now that he was sitting next to me. He saw me looking at it, so he took it away from me.

"Hey!" I exclaimed rather loudly. "Give it back." I tried to argue, but he didn't return my sketchbook. He turned around and flew through the pages of my sketchbook. I never wrote down anything we did in English class. I just listened and sketched.

"Are these yours?" he asked, kind of surprised.

"No, they belong to Jesus," I answered sarcastically as I gave up on trying to get my sketchbook back.

Kai chuckled. "For a nerd, you have quite an attitude."

"For a bad boy wannabe, you have quite an ego," I replied in annoyance. He smiled and shook his head while continuing to turn the pages. I looked at Diana and Addie for help, but those two just stared at the boy next to me like he was a beautiful, almost godlike creature. One thing was for certain, they sure weren't used to me getting the attention.

Kai suddenly stopped and looked at the photo of the school's football team. He was on it too.

"Why do you have this?" He raised his eyebrows. "Don't tell me you're obsessed with me." He smirked. "Don't be embarrassed. I mean, what's not to like?" He winked, and I rolled my eyes.

"Excuse me, Mr. Big Ego, but you're an idiot."

I was embarrassed to admit, but the only reason I had the photo was because Matt looked cute. His smile on that photo was his one-thousand-watt smile he sent to me only when they won a game, but it was also the one he sent every cute girl he saw, which was never me. Maybe I kept the photo all this time because I still had some unresolved feelings for him, hoping that he would send me that smile one day. I knew I was a hopeless case, though.

"Yeah, but I could be your idiot," Kai said flirtatiously with a wink.

"In your dreams," I replied and wanted to smack myself.

"That's why sleeping is my favourite activity next to pleasing you, sweetheart," he said, and this time, I did hit his shoulder and not even *that* gently. Kai knew very well that he was getting into my nerves. Maybe it was something he liked doing, but it was growing old.

The Bad Boy wanted to say something else, yet he was cut off by our as usual *very late* teacher who came in and finally started the class. I got the sketchbook back from him and continued to draw something for Diana's birthday. It wasn't for months to come, but I liked to be sure I got a gift rather than rush at the last minute.

Kai watched me draw, slumping back in his seat, sitting as comfortable as possible, and sometimes even giving a few remarks that I tried badly to ignore. He sat so widely, his left leg touched my right. I think he was actually doing that on purpose because he knew I couldn't move my chair any farther away from him. There was sadly nowhere else to go.

My mission to ignore him was a total fail. After just a few times he nudged my elbow, I got irritated and hissed, "What?"

"Nothing," he said, smirking with his hands up in mock defeat. Only now did I notice he had dimples. Oh my God. Dimples were my secret weakness. Suddenly, Kai became much, much hotter. So totally hot, I was staring. Of course, I hastily looked away, but he still wouldn't give up. I was almost done with my drawing when I felt Kai lean in and whisper something in my ear. I jumped, taken completely off guard.

He said, "You look cute when you're trying to ignore me."

My heart sped up from the proximity and because of his words.

"Tell me something I don't know," I replied, confused by my sudden pretend confidence. There was an inner voice inside my head that tried to snap me out of it. I wasn't going crazy over Kai Asher. The only reason I was reacting this way was because I never got any kind of attention like this.

Oh, who are you kidding? You're at stage one: denial, a little voice said in my head.

"Are you going to the game next Friday?" Kai asked me. I got chills when he asked me that question. Everybody knew that he was a player. He changed girls every single game, and the ones he wanted to *do*, he invited to a game. But clearly, he wasn't inviting me. He was just asking.

"Nah, it's not my thing," I told him. I didn't like football games. There was too much screaming, and I considered it a waste of time since I could be reading or studying instead.

"How come? Your brother plays. Aren't you like twins or something?" he asked.

Oh, so he knew I was Connor's sister.

I felt so stupid. Of course, he knew I was his sister since Connor was involved in that car accident yesterday too. Besides, we shared the same last name. However, I never dared to imagine he knew who I was. I mean, I was an unimportant loser. Actually, I was pretty happy thinking he didn't know who I was.

"Yeah, but it doesn't mean we like the same things. Besides, going to the game would make me spend time with his friends. Don't get me wrong, they're okay. Well, some of them anyway. But I still want to keep my sanity, and the only way to do that is to stay away."

Kai smirked like he knew something I didn't.

"What?" I asked.

"Nothing," he replied.

"What?" I asked again, slightly annoyed.

The bell rang, and he was out of sight before I could say Oreos.

Chapter 5

Two hours later, I was on my way to the cafeteria when I suddenly remembered I needed something urgently from my locker. So I turned around like a lost puppy and wandered around school until I stopped a few meters away at the sight before me.

Addie was talking to a boy, someone who used to be my tutor a few years ago, and it was surprising because they were two different people. She was popular, and he was a loner. Most people considered that to be a social catastrophe, but Addie obviously didn't care. She hung out with me, anyway. I didn't even know why this meant so much to me. The change in the social ladder, I mean.

Not that I cared about popularity. The last thing I wanted was for people to pry into my personal life. Anyways, I pretended to be busy with pulling books out of my bag while Addie and Reese talked, but then I came over, anyway. She was laughing at something he had said before I greeted them.

"Hey, guys," I said before they stepped away from the locker, leaving some space for me to open it.

"Oh, hi, Astrid." He smiled, but he was looking at my best friend, of course. I wondered when he was going to ask her out.

Diana and I knew he liked her, but they never talked so out in the open before.

"I'm just going to get my books, and I'll be out of your way," I said, laughing under my breath. They looked like they were in love and seemed really cute together. Addie with her high heels was just as tall as Reese in his sneakers.

Reese was the kind of guy who won over everyone using only his charm. He was sweet and had dimples, and like I mentioned before, I would die for dimples. He moved from Australia five years back but kept his accent.

"Oh, that's okay. We're just heading out," Adelaide told me.

"Heading out? You know we have two more periods, right?"

Addie never ditched without Diana, but she didn't want to ditch so she could pick me up this morning. I felt a little backstabbed. I needed their help, and they weren't there. So I had to go and hitch a ride on *Kai Asher's* motorcycle to get to school, and I had to endure all those people talking about me. People still gave me stares all because *they* couldn't come pick me up with their little excuse.

"Reese and I are going to Starbucks," she explained. My gaze slipped over to Reese who was watching me intently like I would give something away. I forced my face to remain blank.

"Okay, I'll hold down the fort. You guys have fun and drive safely," I ordered them as I slammed the locker shut, feeling happy for her at the same time before I headed to the cafeteria. Today, we had mini pancakes, and we could choose to eat them with either jam, Nutella or sugar. All very unhealthy, all very delicious. I chose Nutella and coconut flour which was my all-time favourite combo.

As I got my food, Diana called me. I walked to her table and set down my tray before taking out a new book that I was currently reading. While I ate and read, Diana flicked through pages of a *Celebrity Gossip* magazine, a pretty popular magazine in our town.

We spent our lunch breaks like that every single day. I read a book. Diana flipped through her magazine, and Addie was the one studying. It was kind of a routine that I would not change for the world. Being stuck in a book while at school made me feel a little less panicky about being surrounded by people. It helped me deal with my anxiety.

My friends were pretty cool about it too. They didn't give me a hard time for reading books. We supported each other's passions. Addie, Diana, and I might have been very different, but that's what made our friendship so special. The differences between us brought new interesting experiences to our lives.

I was so lost in the world of literature that a tap on my shoulder downright startled me. I looked up to see my brother that never wanted to be seen with me in school because he found out what kind of a burden I was. But then again, I supposed he heard about Kai and me this morning and wanted to have a talk. I sighed and scooted over so he could sit down at the table.

Suddenly, without warning, Matt, Nathaniel, and Beck sat down at the table. It started to become crowded. Diana attempted to contradict, but no one cared. Soon enough, they were all over us and not in a good way.

"So, Astrid," Matt said to me. I hated his attitude. Any time he talked to me, he was rude or just a jerk. "Found a new, less boring way to spend your days?"

"Screw you, Matt," I said and tried to read my book. He chuckled like I said something funny.

"You're stuck in books like your life depends on it. Maybe if you stopped being such a nerd and made attempts at conversation, people would actually like you."

"Can I punch him?" Diana asked me, getting slightly angry.

"Maybe if you kept your dick in your pants, you wouldn't spread any diseases around the school. Then again, you're like bacteria. You go around, and everybody tries to get rid of you," I said back, trying not to be bothered by his attempts to hurt me. I had no idea why he said any of these things, but I got so used to it by now that it didn't bother me to be mean back.

He really hurt me a couple of years ago when I liked him. He always treated me like trash lying on the sidewalk. He broke my heart, and I was never right afterwards.

"Oh, she burned you." Beck started to laugh at Matt who only smirked and looked at me with a certain interest in his eyes. I raised an eyebrow, but he didn't look away.

"How have you been?" he asked finally, and it shocked me. Connor kept quiet, eating his sandwich and checking out girls that passed our table.

"Um, good?" I said, unable to figure out what he was up to. I focused my attention to Diana who shrugged.

"That's great. Cindy would love to hear that." He smiled in mischief, probably because he knew I used to like him and hate her. "Ever thought of getting a boyfriend? Oh right, nobody wants to even look at you."

"Matt, that's enough!" Connor snapped at him. "That's my sister, and you'll show some respect."

"I don't need you defending me." I turned to Connor though I was glad he chose to do it. I tried not to let Matt's words have an effect on me, but what he said was a low blow.

Connor looked at me as if I was crazy, but I held my ground. I hated that everybody thought picking on me was okay because I was helpless anyway and not strong enough to defend myself. They must have thought I was weak. Sometimes, they were right, but not today. I would not let Matt get to me.

Everything was going bad, but I was going to grit my teeth and get through this day. At least until I got home and throw myself into books to forget all my pain.

"What are you guys even doing here?" Diana asked them, trying to find out why their sudden visit actually happened.

"Oh, just hanging out. Catching up with you. Things like that," Beck said before anyone else could speak. Connor's stare was intense, and I couldn't shake it off. I wanted to get out of here because I didn't have an appetite anymore. I knew my brother was mad, curious even, but I didn't want to go through his inquisition. I decided to turn the tables around.

"Well, I can tell you now that nothing's new. Anyways, isn't hanging out with me an embarrassment? Am I not a loser enough for you to stay away? You don't want to ruin your reputation and all," I spoke.

"Why would you say that?" Nathaniel asked, confused. He was always the nice one. He was my closest guy friend. Connor and Matt looked at each other, and a look passed between them.

"Heard it so many times from you now. I just assumed you didn't want to be around me any more than necessary," I said and started to gather my stuff. "So I'll do you a favour and leave."

Diana sent me a worried look, and I guess she knew I was in one of my moods now, the mood that was close to breaking down. I chose to ignore her.

Then before I could get away, the guys from the rest of the football team decided to join us at the table, but it was too small, so they carried other free tables to ours and put them together. I wanted to run away, and my anxiety made me fidget in my seat.

I put the book in my purse and took the half-eaten food on my tray and gave it to Connor who was clearly hungry. I stood up to leave when Kai strode into the cafeteria. He had a perky blonde dancing around him the whole time it took him to walk to our table. I ignored him deliberately. Diana said something about giving her some notes, so I hurriedly searched my bag for them as Kai neared us.

"There's no place for two," Matt said, clearly suggesting that he should get rid of the girl. Kai waved her off, and while she sounded clearly hurt, she still gave him a kiss.

"Bye, baby. See ya later." She winked at him. After her departure, Kai went to grab his lunch and decided to sit down next to Diana. I gave her the notes and wanted to leave right away, but Kai decided to speak to me.

"Why are you in such a hurry to get away, princess? Don't like hanging out with the cool people?" he asked, taking a bite off his sandwich.

"If by cool you mean silly airheads, then I am surprised why anyone would want to be in your company," I replied. He smiled and nodded.

"Some of them might be a little slow, but they're talented when it comes to sports. You can't deny that," Kai said. I had no idea why I kept standing by their table when I could have left already.

"If only their egos weren't so inflated," I responded and pointed my stare at Matt who seemed to be a little confused by what was happening.

"See? You're so fun to talk to. Why don't you sit down and be my company? You can ignore anyone that has a big ego by your special standards," he spoke.

"Does that mean I can ignore you?" I asked with a sweet smile.

"I'm too incredible to be ignored," he said with a laugh and motioned for me to sit down. I groaned and sat down with some effort.

"Don't be so daft," I retorted. I saw people giving us surprised looks, probably wondering how could Kai Asher, of all people, convince me to sit back down when I so obviously wanted to get away. Deep down, I was wondering the same thing.

"You need a ride home?" Matt asked. I think it was the first time he ever showed me kindness, but I was not foolish enough to believe it.

"No, thanks. I'll manage," I said, not wanting his help at all since I knew it came with a price.

"But wasn't Addie supposed to give you a ride today?" Diana asked.

"I have plans," I simply said. They couldn't argue with that, could they?

Connor laughed. "Plans? You?" He laughed some more.

Apparently, they could, I thought to myself. "Yes," I said angrily. "Is that so hard to believe or are you just a self-absorbed asshole?"

"Oh, yeah? With whom then?" Connor said as if testing me.

Suddenly, a voice said, "With me."

It was Kai.

Chapter 6

Everybody at the table fell silent. I stared at Kai, trying to figure out his game. I left quickly after the whole scene ended and headed to my biology classroom. Kai appeared next to me. I almost didn't see him, but I heard his footsteps.

"Why do you look so pissed?" he asked cautiously.

"Why did you do that?" I snapped at him. It wasn't intentional. I just didn't like owing people.

"Do what? Help you?" He ran a hand through his hair, making him damn hotter than he already was. There was confusion in his brown eyes.

"No. Why did you lie?" I asked.

"Because I thought your brother was an asshole and that he deserved a decent surprise on his hands. He needs to learn not to underestimate you." Kai defended his actions, and I did understand what he was trying to say even though he hardly knew me. "Besides, I ruined your car, so I thought I'd make it up to you by saving you from walking *or* going with Matt."

"Why do you even care?" I stopped in the middle of an empty hallway to meet his eyes.

"Sweetheart." He sighed. "I may be arrogant, and I may be a player, but I also moved next to your house, and I plan on fulfilling my duties as a good neighbour."

"Bullshit," I blurted out.

"Okay, I feel guilty about causing the accident. It was my fault, and I admit it. I'm sorry, okay? So would you just let me help you for once?"

"I don't like it when people help me," I said in all honesty.

"I can see that. You're your own person, and I respect that. You hate interaction from what I can see, and you like to be left alone, but sometimes, even the best people need to admit they need a hand."

I hesitated with my reply because I didn't know what to say. "I'm going to say this once, so don't expect me to say it again…but thank you."

He smiled, and I believed it was sincere this time. "Of course. Now let's go, or we're going to be late, princess."

Kai escorted me to my locker and talked about little meaningless things to entertain me. Then we walked to biology class that we had together and split up once we were inside the classroom.

I sat down next to my friend Delilah. She was one of the nicest girls and a really close friend of mine. We were always partners in bio because both of us were good at it and hated being paired up with people who made us do all the work. It wasn't fair because, in the end, they got the same grade as us for the project we did. That was why Delilah and I were together—to split the work equally and have fun in doing so.

"Hey there, Delilah," I said, cheerfully quoting the song. She smiled widely as she waited for me to sit down. Kai disappeared into the classroom, and I didn't care where he was. Being around Delilah made me feel a bit better.

"Hey, Astrid. What's up? How was your weekend?"

"It was fine. I read a lot, ate unhealthy food, and danced around the house in my PJs. Nothing more exciting." I was sarcastic at the last part, but Delilah giggled.

"I would kill to see your dance moves at my party after the game," she said, and I was surprised to be invited. Most people didn't bother inviting me because a nerd like me had no right to be there or would never show up, anyway.

"I'll think about it," I spoke with a little uncertainty.

"If you don't want to come alone, you can always bring Addie and Diana with you."

I smiled nicely before changing the subject. "How was *your* weekend?"

"It was certainly less exciting than yours. I had family dinners to attend and game nights to suffer through, and let's not talk about yesterday," she told me.

"I agree. My day was really boring yesterday." I thought about what I had done that day and everything I accomplished. It was nothing. I hadn't done anything productive since I slept through the whole day.

I heard someone having a coughing seizure behind us and turned to see Kai. Delilah sent him a weird look and asked him if he was okay.

"I'm fine. I just have something stuck in my throat. Probably from the food I ate *yesterday*," Kai said, looking over at me, and I knew he was insulted by my comment. Apparently, he didn't consider yesterday so uninteresting.

Delilah turned to me and whispered with a shake of her head, "Boys."

I could feel Kai's gaze on me the entire time even when I had my back turned to him. His partner kept hitting on him the whole time, and I couldn't hear the teacher because she wouldn't shut up. I was so frustrated by the end of the first period. The teacher ended up having some problems with the computer, and some samples were missing, but the next one we had, she started picking out the pairs we worked in.

"Kora Portland and Sam Cross, the front row." Mrs. Aldrin pointed at the table they would be sitting for rest of the year.

"Annaleigh Jefferson and Rachel Peters, second row next to the window." The two girls moved. A couple more were named until very few of us were left.

"Kai Asher…Oh, we have a problem here. You seem to be failing this class already. If you don't get a better grade this term, I'm afraid you'll have to go to summer school," she told him.

"Yeah, I'm working on that. You see, my friend Astrid Bailey promised to help me out," Kai spoke.

"No, I didn't," I objected.

"I think that's a wonderful idea," Mrs. Aldrin said.

"But I can't help him. I have to study for my own classes and—"

"I understand, but consider how good it would look on your college application," Mrs. Aldrin interjected, knowing this would get me to reconsider. And damn it, she was right. It was just the kind of thing I needed—the kind of thing I was looking for, the thing that was missing.

I groaned really loudly, just to point out how much I hated this. "Fine."

"Great. You two can sit in the back row, next to the window. Talk quietly while working. Astrid, explain things to him as you go so he can catch up sooner," she instructed, and I sighed as I followed Kai to the back of the class.

"You should've asked me if I was okay with this first before you decided to bring this up," I said in displeasure.

"But I thought tutoring me is every girl's dream." Kai smiled innocently as I gave him a pointed look.

"Whatever. Let's get this done."

Chapter 7

I explained some things to Kai who, I learned, either used to sleep through all the work or not pay attention to anything we did in this class. Ten minutes before class ended, Kai offered to drive me home.

"I don't think that will be necessary." I tried to turn him down gently. I didn't know what it was, but I really hated riding his bike. Motorcycles were not my thing. They suited him, though.

I admitted to myself that Kai wasn't necessarily that bad, but people still stared when I was around him. Then again, I was getting a bit used to it, and his constant attempts at conversation were a wonderful distraction.

"Come on, Astrid." He tried to convince me. "It's okay to be scared. Just know that I'm here, okay?" He took my hand teasingly which made me roll my eyes, but I couldn't help smiling a bit.

"I'd rather walk, really," I replied.

"Connor believes you're going with me, princess. What would he think if he saw you walking home alone?" I had to admit that Kai had a point. He would laugh at me because he honestly didn't believe I could have plans.

"Fine." I gave in with reluctance.

"Can you slow down? I need to get to my locker first," I told Kai because as soon as class ended, he grabbed my arm and led me through the hallways to avoid peoples' stares. He found out pretty quickly how much that bothered me, which I also hated.

I made my way to the locker and opened it. Taped on the inside was a picture of me, Addie, Vanessa, and Diana from a few years ago. I loved that picture because we were all smiling, and the lighting was so perfect, you couldn't help but love it.

It was also the only picture I had with Vanessa that turned out to be actually cute. Seeing it every time made my heart ache. I missed her so much. She died in a plane crash.

Surrounding that picture were shirtless magazine cutouts of our top ten hottest actors. Kai looked at me when he saw them and raised an eyebrow.

"You have a problem?" I asked, amused by his surprise. He chuckled and shook his head in disbelief.

I put my books in and slammed it shut before turning to Kai when my heart nearly stopped. We were barely two feet apart. I stepped back before anything could happen, then turned on my heels and walked out.

Dear Diary,

It was a new day—Friday, to be exact—and I was having lunch in the cafeteria with my brother and his friends. They suddenly made it a habit to irritate me. I was incredibly shy because of the crowd and didn't say anything at first, but then they started asking me questions about school and all sorts of things. It was hard to be comfortable, but I felt proud that a part of me got used to the feeling and that I was able to respond without stuttering.

Kai ignored me practically all day. Not that I was complaining. He insisted on giving me a ride to school this morning, and I said no. He wouldn't give up, so we got into an argument, and it ended with him being all sulky. I had no idea what made him speak to me in the first place.

My parents didn't want to buy me a new car even though we had more than enough money. We weren't, like, horribly rich. We just had more money than we could ever possibly need—or so was my opinion. My mom and dad worked long hours. Dad was a lawyer, and Mom was a nurse. They weren't home a lot.

I was a little cold today since I forgot to take my jacket with me. By the time we had lunch, I couldn't feel any of my fingers.

"I can't believe I forgot about that physics homework. Mr. Peterson's going to kill me," I mumbled to myself while searching through my bag. I felt so stupid because I double-checked to make sure I had everything ready for today, and this still happened.

"You're too big a nerd. Are you sure there's nothing wrong with you?" Matt commented. He was still an asshat to me, and no amount of time we spend together would change that.

"I don't know. I probably got the stupidity syndrome from you, Matt," I replied to his lame comment and left my bag alone. I ended up picking at my food. Today's lunch options were very plain and just downright gross, but the cafeteria was lively. All around the school were posters and banners for the game.

Everybody was excited about it. Football was the biggest, most important thing in this school, but because I was useless at sports, I wanted to join the choir. My mom pushed me to go to

Broadway since we had connections, but I didn't have enough courage. That would be a humongous step, and it was too big for me. Besides, performing in front of a crowd was a big no-no.

There was a phase where she wanted to send me off to New York and attend the Music Boarding School. My aunt was actually the principal, which was really cool. I mean, I knew I was good at singing; I just didn't want everybody else to know it too. It was my special little thing.

When Di and Addie finished eating, we stood up to leave. I was almost at the door of the cafeteria when I heard Beck shout my name. He jogged over and slipped off his jersey. "Here, take this. You look like you're freezing," he said and handed it over. I looked up at him, eyebrow raised. He knew I was cold.

"You can give it back to me later."

I nodded shyly and thanked him.

Chapter 8

Hey Diary,

I still have mixed feelings about writing to you because it feels a bit weird, though I have to admit writing is becoming a therapy for me. I spent most of my time in my room after I came home and watched a movie before going to bed.

The weekend almost passed without any complications *until* Kai rang the doorbell. Connor had a date with some girl, and my parents weren't home as per usual. There was only me left to answer the door. So imagine a half-asleep Astrid Ella Bailey, in her knee-high socks, some ridiculous shorts, and a Thor shirt on and then him looking like a god, standing in front of me as graceful as ever. If that wasn't enough to wake me up, then I didn't know what was.

"Kai? Do you know what time it is?" I asked sleepily, scratching my head, fingers slightly tangling between my hair.

"Yeah, it's eleven AM. Get dressed, sleepy head," he said, striding through the doorway and inviting himself in.

"Why?" I was unsure, and being woken up was not something I appreciated on a Saturday. It was the only day I slept in.

"I'm taking you to breakfast, and then you'll help me study bio," he said as a matter-of-fact.

"It's too early for this." I grunted but still went to my room. I quickly got dressed, and we left for the diner where I ordered two toasts with a strawberry milkshake. Kai had eggs and bacon, which was apparently his favourite thing to eat for breakfast.

"So," Kai started the conversation. "Truth or dare?"

"Truth," I said without even having to think twice. Kai smirked, and I immediately regretted my decision.

"What's the deal between you and Matt?" Kai asked.

"What do you mean?"

"Oh, you two just seem to have this unspeakable tension between each other." Kai observed.

It was true. Matt and I were never fully comfortable around each other. "If you hadn't noticed by now, he's an asshole."

"What did you do to get him so pissed?"

"Me? I didn't do anything. Even as kids, he treated me like trash on the sidewalk. He's never been nice," I told Kai, but I looked down at my food.

"I'm sorry about that, really. But I'm glad you are able to stand up to him and put him in his place. I know it's not my place to say, but I'm proud," Kai said to me, and I frowned.

"Why would you be proud of that?" I took a bite from my toast.

"Because out of all things you seem to be afraid of doing, of all the things holding you back, you're not afraid to defend yourself." I didn't know what to say, so I just shrugged. "Besides, your conversations are entertaining. Who would've thought Connor Bailey's little sister was so feisty." He smirked, but it looked like he wanted to say something else.

"Don't call me that." I corrected him. "Connor is only older than me by minutes, but that doesn't mean he's more mature. I swear the idiot acts like a five-year-old kid sometimes."

"Noted," he replied. "I have to tell you something," Kai said and hesitated for a moment before spilling out what was on his mind. "Well, you know how everyone sat down at your table in the cafeteria? It's because Connor and Matt wanted to hang out for old time's sake, whatever that means."

"It's their term for picking on me," I explained. "They always called it that."

"Do you want me to help you deal with them?" Kai asked, and I found myself wondering when I started having a conversation this civil with him.

"No, that's okay. They'll grow bored sooner or later." I lied.

"Are you sure? Or are you saying no just because you don't like people helping you?"

"I'm sure, Kai. Why do you even want to help me?"

"Because I feel as if you're stuck in your bubble, and everybody keeps trying to poke it with a stick to see when it pops," he said.

"After seventeen years of living with Connor, I got used to it."

"You shouldn't have to get used to it, you know?"

"Connor's been through a lot. We both deal with grief our own way. So if his is picking on me, then so be it. At the end of the day, it distracts me from my own." I explained. Kai didn't ask what I was talking about because I guess he felt he didn't have a right. So I changed the subject.

"I imagined you'd be way more intense like the rest of the popular guys from school. They're always so serious, and sometimes even though they're popular, it's easier to see through their shell than through anybody else's. The more you try to be something you're not, the more you become see-through."

"That's...unbelievably true. But I mean, everybody has their own problems. I just happen to ignore mine," Kai stated.

"And how's that working for ya?" I teased him with a smile.

"It went fine until I failed this really important biology pop quiz, and now, I'm choosing not to ignore the problem anymore so I can solve it." He looked up from his plate, and I remembered that this was the only reason why he wanted me here, anyway. It wasn't like he wanted my company.

My smile faded, and I became serious again. "Good thing I can help you out then," I said, and we ate. After that, we went to his house to study. It was the first time I was there.

"My parents are with my little sister Hannah, so they're not going to be home for hours."

I nodded but felt insecure being alone with him in his house. I knew that we weren't going to do anything other than study, but it felt weird. I guess I trusted him enough to be alone with him. Besides, if he turned out to be a mass murderer, I could just run into my house and call 911.

Kai's home was huge and identical to mine, only the furniture was different. His bedroom was darker. Unlike my brother, he had movie posters up. I noticed that all the movie posters he had were of book-to-movie adaptations.

And then I noticed a bookshelf in the corner of his room. Without even having to tell my feet to move, I slid across the room, and my fingers brushed the spines of his books.

"I didn't know you read." I looked at him wide-eyed, and he gave me a shy smile.

"I…um." He cleared his throat. "I do it when I need to chill out." Kai looked uncomfortable, and it took me a few moments to figure out why that was.

The Bad Boy was secretly a bookworm. And here I was thinking how cute that was—or dare I say, sexy. Yes, I found people who liked to read very sexy.

"Don't worry. I won't tell," I said to Kai, eyeing his books, and I heard a sigh of relief. I smiled to myself. Who would've thought Kai Asher liked to read?

My fingers skimmed across the covers of his books. Amongst other books, he had *Lord of the Rings, Eragon, Harry Potter, The Hunger Games, Divergent, I Am Number Four,* and *The Maze Runner.*

I was shocked by how similar our tastes were.

I turned to him, remembering why I was here. "Anyways, we should probably study." He handed me his books, and then I realized that Kai *really* needed help.

He didn't know the first thing about cells, or the human organs, or the blood types, or anything in general. And every time I tried to teach him something, he would either scoot closer or change the subject.

I knew it was a subconscious move, but that also meant Kai and I had to meet more often, and I had no idea whether to jump from happiness or cry my eyes out.

Chapter 9

Diary dearest,

I do regret to inform you that Kai and I hadn't talked much after that day. Well, I don't really regret it, to be honest. The reason we didn't talk was because he was busy with football practices and he ditched a lot of his classes, but we still had plans to meet up this Sunday so I could tutor him. The few times I saw him was when he hung out with other girls, and I saw him take two on a date, but that was never my business.

There was an awkward moment when I just got to my room, and he didn't have his curtains closed. I could see them going at it. I cringed so bad and shut mine. With the end of the last class I had on Friday, I planned to go home, do my homework, and study for the math exam we had next month.

Which was exactly what I did. I asked my two best friends to drop me off at home after we stopped by Starbucks first. We hung out for about one hour, and when we got home, Connor wasn't there. He had football practice with the rest of his team, being the captain and all.

So, the girls and I just went to my room where I went through my closet, showing them the new clothes I bought a few days ago.

"Oh, I like that one," Diana said, taking a dress from my hands to admire it a bit closer. Addie nodded in approval while we chatted about meaningless things.

"I think we need to go shopping some more. Not counting the new clothes you bought, your closet is screaming for attention," Diana told me, and I laughed.

"I know. I just couldn't find the time to go shopping nowadays. Besides, I hate going alone." I put back the dress Diana handed over and sighed.

"You can always call us. We can make some time for shopping. Besides, we haven't hung out much lately since you're so busy and Kai seems to take up most of your time." Addie insinuated with a smile and exchanged a look with Diana.

"That's not true. Kai and I hadn't spent time together in forever, and when we do, I tutor him. That's *all*."

"If you say so. Oh, did you two hear about what happened in the changing rooms?" Addie snapped her fingers as if she almost forgot to tell me.

"No, what happened?" Di asked, plopping down on a chair.

"There was a fight between the guys two weeks ago. A bet spiralled out of control, or so I heard," Addie said, her black hair sprawled all over my pillow as her eyes stared at my ceiling.

"Really?" I questioned, getting slightly curious. Addie nodded but didn't look at me as she continued.

"Why are we hearing about that now if it happened two weeks ago?" Diana asked her.

"Because the bet was supposed to be a secret. It's about one guy—I don't know who yet—trying to get a girl in his bed by the end of school year. My sources tell me that he's failing horribly because the girl is apparently the most hard to get girl in school and also not one people would usually talk to."

"Do you know any names?" Diana asked, but Addie shook her head. That was strange. Addie always knew everything.

"As I said, the guys are keeping it a secret so that the bet would be fair. But there's a lot of money placed into it and apparently threats too. The bet drove a wedge in the team, and one person told me some punches were thrown in as well."

"Wow, that's really strange. Which girl could make the guys fight like that?" I asked, not really getting why anyone would fight over a girl. Nobody would fight for me, anyway, so maybe that's why I was one-sided.

"Don't know, but she must be pretty special if you ask me," Diana said then motioned for me to go through more clothes.

I didn't care about the fight or the bet since that was between the guys, and I didn't give two shits about their fights.

"Addie, darling, how was your"—I coughed intentionally—"coffee with Reese?" Diana caught on quickly, and a smile played on her lips as well. She turned her blue eyes into Addie's direction, and ladies and gentlemen, it was the first time in fourteen years I saw Adelaide Torrins blush. It was sweet.

"It went okay," she said quietly, but Addie was not the kind of person to be quiet. That was my job. Addie was the stubborn, honest one. Diana was the talkative party girl. I was the sometimes hostile, anti-social person in our clique, and I didn't have any problem with it. In fact, I liked to own up to it.

"Just okay?" Diana pushed for details.

"No, not just okay. It was ah-may-zing!" she said dreamily. "*He* was amazing. Reese was sweet and funny. He paid for my coffee and everything. He listened to everything I said, and he seemed genuinely interested in what I thought about it." She had to catch her breath before continuing. "Guys, I think I might have a slightly huge crush on him."

Diana squealed and rushed towards Adelaide to hug her. Addie was shocked but hugged her back. I smiled to myself. All I wanted was for my friend to be happy, and I knew they couldn't ignore each other's feelings forever. Also, the sight of my two best friends hugging made me slightly sentimental.

"That's great," Diana spoke.

"I'm happy for you, Addie," I told her.

"So, are you two together now?" Di asked, and after that question, a ton more followed.

We passed the time by talking about my trip to the Winterheart bookstore and my latest book haul. I talked about Patch Cipriano who was one of my favourite fictional bad boys in history right next to Daemon Black. The topic switched to the latest fashion trends, and Diana talked about what her favourite celebrities did for the past week. Hours had passed before Addie and Di made a quick stop at their houses to get ready.

We were planning on attending the game. Both of my best friends decided they would drag me against my will if they had to, and then there was the after party at Delilah's.

While they were gone, I decided on my outfit and matched it with my makeup. As I waited for them to come pick me up, I went downstairs to play the piano for a while. Our living room was quite big, and I still remembered that even as a child, my mom would teach me how to play. We would spend our days trying to come up with new songs we dedicated to special people in our lives. It became our thing.

Then the doorbell rang, and I was snapped out of my reverie. My best friends were waiting outside for me. They looked gorgeous, and I knew, without a doubt, I wouldn't be leaving with them tonight. They'd probably ditch me, and I would have to walk or something.

I tried to shrug off my bad vibes before going to the car. Tonight, I would get to see Connor play and support him, which was something I hadn't done in a while.

A part deep inside me was starting to get excited about the game.

Chapter 10

Dear Diary,

We took Diana's car to the game, and the moment we arrived, cheers and shouts could be heard all around. I remembered to take Beck's jersey with me so I could return it.

As soon as we got there, my two best friends were eating all the attention up. People turned to us and to me as well, in surprise. I never showed up at any of the games and everybody knew my relationship with Connor was complex. Football was his thing, and going to the games would mean I supported him—something he never wanted, needed, or asked for.

I heard occasional whispers and felt quite uncomfortable. Scanning the crowd for Beck, I remembered that he was in the boy's locker room with the rest of the team preparing for the game.

Addie found us some empty seats, and they dragged me into the crowd. One person stopped to talk to me. "Finally decided to grow some balls and come, huh, loser?"

I think some of the girls were so in love with Connor that they thought my relationship with him was all up in their business.

They took a special interest in it, and I often got harassed by his stalkers. Which was another thing that drove a wedge between us.

Heat rushed to my cheeks, and before I could think of a response, Diana and Addie stepped in front of me.

"Call her a loser one more time, and we'll make sure you won't have any teeth left." Diana threatened.

"And we'll also pop those fake boobs," Addie added before walking away with me.

I thanked both of them, and they squeezed my hands.

"Nobody messes with us," Diana replied. I ended up checking out who else came to the game. It seemed most people there were going to my school plus some parents. I wondered if Kai's parents came. I never met them.

The music blasted through the field as we waited for the game to start. Diana got us some drinks, and I welcomed the cold beverage. A few moments later, the music stopped, and the cheering began. The players ran onto the field, and soon, the game began. I saw Connor first, then I recognized Nathaniel by his way of walking or should I say running. Matt looked completely focused on the game, but Beck seemed out of it. Our eyes locked for a moment, and he smiled at me.

I didn't see Kai anywhere, and after a time-out or whatever the sports term was—I really didn't follow any sports—most of the players disappeared. I quickly broke away to head to the restroom. The game continued, and though I was bored as hell, I watched my brother play amazingly. He really was a star, and he deserved a football scholarship at the best college.

It was no surprise that we won, but it had made everyone more excited than they already were. I pushed through the crowd to get to my brother and Beck. When Connor saw me, he looked surprised, if not shocked.

"Astrid, what are you doing here?" he asked me. I was uncomfortable with all the attention that I got and wanted to shrink back immediately.

"What? I can't take some time off studying to see my brother be the football star that he is?" I asked innocently.

"Okay, you're right about me being the football star, but I know you hate football, so why are you here?" He raised one eyebrow in suspicion.

"Di and Addie insisted. Plus, I have to return Beck's jersey. He lent it to me a while ago, and I wasn't able to give it back before," I said and handed the jersey over to him. Beck was smiling as I thanked him.

Suddenly, a crowd of team players ran up to us and hugged each other, congratulating themselves on another great game.

"Astrid, you look amazing!" Nathaniel complimented me, and I blushed shyly.

"Thank you, Nath. You're sweet." I hugged him even though he was smelly. Then again, they all were, and I was surrounded by everyone.

"You guys were unbelievable out there," Diana said, twisting her hair in between her fingers.

"We were, weren't we?" Matt said, and some of them laughed. I just rolled my eyes at his arrogant, cocky, egotistical, self-centred reply. I could go on all day. "Good to see you finally showed up and did something interesting for a while." He took a cheap shot at me.

"And that is?"

"Watching me play," he said, and I scoffed.

"As if that's anything impressive. If anything, Connor's the real deal," I snapped, and Connor smiled proudly before putting an arm around my shoulder.

"See that? That's my sister," he gushed, and I rolled my eyes, but I was pleasantly surprised by his sweetness. Never had he said I was his sister in a good way. He always meant it as complaint or insult.

"Shouldn't you guys go and change?" Addie asked, and I heard my name being called out. I turned to Delilah, who was jogging to meet us. She was pushing through the crowd of players and finally came to a halt in front of me.

"Hey, Astrid." She hugged me before turning to my friends, "Adelaide, Diana." The girls gave her a nod, and Delilah turned back to me. "You coming to the party?"

"Yeah, I am." There was a smile on my face before Connor sent me a weird look. I knew he didn't like me being friends with Delilah, as she was an extremely open person, unafraid to do anything. She didn't care what people thought, and she did whatever she wanted. She sometimes convinced me to go out of my comfort zone, and there was nothing I could say to thank her for it. Sure, it was uncomfortable, but if I didn't have her, I would still be stuck in my room unable to go to school and socialize with people because of my anxiety.

She helped me a lot and let me know she was always there by my side. I liked that she didn't gossip about others, and most of the time, she defended people. She was a loyal friend, and I admired that about her. Delilah, my girls, and I fell into conversation as soon as the guys left. I glanced around the stadium when Adelaide and Diana were busy asking Delilah about her outfit when my eyes landed on *him*.

Still in his uniform, with a girl around him kissing him passionately, stood Kai. It wasn't the girl that day at lunch. I guess she was pretty too. I liked her brown hair.

I looked away for a moment when Delilah asked me a question. When I answered half-heartedly, I looked back and met his gaze. He was watching me intently like he wanted to say something. I felt uneasy under his intense gaze, and when he gave me a smile, I smiled back and reminded myself to breathe. It was okay.

Kai left soon to change, and I waited with my girls for Connor. His little girlfriend continued standing there and, every now and again, stared at me with hostility in her eyes. I was grateful when Connor arrived and walked straight over to me. Addie and Diana waited for me at the car while I talked to my brother.

"So," Connor said hesitantly. He looked like a child, which he still was. Something told me he was nervous too. He ran a hand through his brown hair and took a deep breath before saying what was on his mind. "How did you like the game?"

We walked really slowly to the car, taking small steps. I turned to him and smiled. "You know I'm not a fan of football, but you were amazing."

"Thanks, midget," he said, wanting to ruffle my hair, but I slapped his hand away.

There was a short silence that followed.

"So I take it you're going to the party?" I nodded.

"You?"

"I wasn't planning on going, but I changed my mind."

"And let me guess, you're going to keep an eye on me?" He nodded, and I smiled. He was overprotective, and at times, he wasn't all that bad. Especially when he was in this kind of mood. It was rare when I was happy to have him there. I knew parties could seriously trigger my anxiety. One minute, I could be fine, and the other, I'd be sobbing on the floor of the bathroom. He would be there to make sure that didn't happen.

"I can't let you destroy our family reputation," he said, chuckling as we neared the car.

"Says the guy who puked on his girlfriend's shoes," I replied. She was my best friend. While my love for her was infinite, Connor's love for her was more than that. Losing her was hard for both of us. I felt that pain a little more intense than it was a moment ago. I wasn't in the mood to be hanging around with people, but maybe alcohol would let me forget.

We said goodbye. I got into the car and closed the door.

"So, girls. What's up?" I asked. They looked at me and screamed.

"Let's party!"

By the time we arrived there, it was already 11:30 PM, but it was Friday, so no worries. I used to go to parties before she died. At that age, birthday parties and sleepovers were the shiz. Imagine a thirteen-year-old going to high school parties. Yeah, right. I used to have at least a small social life before and was heading higher until I fell harder than Jennifer Lawrence at the Oscars.

The music was blasting through the speakers, and there were teenagers everywhere. It was a house next to the lake with plenty of room. Diana and I started dancing as Addie headed off to greet Reese. Huh, I never knew Reese went to parties. I guess a lot had changed after I stopped going.

Diana whispered in my ear that there were cute guys watching, and I would have normally hidden in an empty room, but this time, I wanted to have some fun. I'd been studying for the past couple of weeks, and I felt the stress getting to me. Addie joined us soon, and we went to sit at the table, which I liked much more.

I had the right to take one night off, and just because I was anti-social, it didn't mean I shouldn't come to parties. I still had the right to go. I just chose not to most of the time.

Our song came on a few minutes later. Addie and Diana practically had to force me on the dance floor again, but I sucked it up and went, anyway. I was glad I did because I ended up relaxing completely as I drank and danced with my friends. Addie and I were both so awkward at dancing which made us laugh so hard. And, Diary, I was having so much fun.

Before the song ended, Diana returned with our drinks, and I happily accepted mine. Delilah came to greet us, and Addie looked behind me. A surprised look was on her face, so I turned around before I saw all the guys from the football team watching me intently. They had never seen me like this—no one had. At times, my shyness changed into a bitchy attitude, and they slowly grew irritated with me. It often resulted in Connor and me fighting, me slamming the door and locking him out. Now, even I didn't know I could be this relaxed after everything that happened.

And by the looks they were giving me, it was clear they thought of me differently now. Kai was there too, with his nothing less than gorgeous little girlfriend for the day shooting daggers at me. Meanwhile, Matt's expression was unreadable.

With a shot in my hand, I winked at my brother and his friends before drinking it and slamming the glass down on the table near me.

As The Cab's song Living Louder started playing, I was lost in the music. I sang with my three favourite girls and just let go for the night.

I probably had too much to drink since I could barely stand straight, much less walk. Addie was completely drunk, and Diana was nowhere to be found. It was one AM, and the party was still fully operational. Up and running. Just going. Raging. Yeah, I was definitely drunk, and I thought everything was a good idea.

Laughing with Addie, I sat down on the front porch, ignoring the crowd around us. There was a good chance they were drunker than us anyways.

"I can't believe you didn't tell me about California," she said in slurred speech, mentioning the summer I spent away from home. "And who's this Luke you mentioned?"

"Wouldn't you like to know?" I said back, laughing mischievously at my best friend. To be honest, I was so drunk. I barely knew who we were talking about by now.

Addie helped both of us stand up again, but I felt an arm around me. As I turned, I saw Connor by my side. "We're going home," he shouted over the loud music that was heard outside.

"Already?" I complained. "But I was having so much fun." Probably too much fun if a person could have too much fun.

"You've had enough fun for tonight. I'm taking you home. No objections," he ordered as he dragged me down the stairs and to the car. I tried to resist, but he was too strong.

"Okay, Dad." I scrambled as much sarcasm into my voice as I could but failed miserably.

"How cute, her sarcastic skills are gone when she's drunk," Matt said as we neared the car. The players were all gathered there, probably saying goodbye. Kai was there too.

"Watch it, Matilda," I replied to Matt's lame comment. It'd been my nickname for him for years, and he hated it. "You might lose whatever's left of your balls. Oh, that's right. You never had any!"

"And you definitely don't want to get on her bad side when she's drunk," Beck added as the guys laughed at my comeback.

"Shut up," I said and kicked him.

"She's violent too. Good thing we're driving her, otherwise she might end up behind bars. Wild animal and all that stuff," Matt said, and I flipped him off.

"You know what? I'll make a special effort to puke in your car tonight."

Matt looked at Connor in panic, not knowing if I was serious or not. I smirked at the asshat, but my legs almost gave out, and Connor had to tighten his grip around me.

"Whoa, Sis," he said. "You okay?"

"I'm fine. Just tired." I snuggled up to him, which he definitely wasn't used to, but I was drunk. I did some crazy things tonight which I would probably regret in the morning. Then again, I could play the I-don't-remember-anything card.

"Right," Nathaniel said. "We should probably get going. See ya on Monday, everyone." The guys all said their goodbyes, but there was one goodbye that made me look up.

It was Kai's. Our eyes met for a moment, and I felt like my breath knocked out of my lungs. The guys hadn't left yet when I started resisting Connor's grip again. He looked so surprised; he let me go for a moment.

"Hey, where are you going?" he asked.

"I want to get drunk." I managed to say.

"You already are drunk," he said.

"I want to get *drunkerrr*," I added.

"No, you don't. Mom's having a dinner tomorrow night, and you don't want to attend it with a hangover."

"Oh God, that's tomorrow?" I groaned.

"Come on, Astrid. We need to go home."

"I want to go with Diana," I protested.

"I forgot how stubborn she is when she's not herself," Matt commented, probably thinking of all the times I was on pills. He stepped in front of me and said, "Come on, little girl. It's time to go home."

He picked me up even with me kicking and managed to get me into the car with the others. Then he slipped into the driver's seat and took me home.

Chapter 11

Dear Diary,

Saturday morning came a lot sooner than it was supposed to. Why? Because my damn new neighbour couldn't keep his music down. Again.

This was seriously starting to get old. I didn't remember getting home. I only remembered falling asleep in the car. Connor must've carried me inside. I felt so tired, and my head was throbbing. Even though I was in a cranky mood, I had no wish to argue with Kai so early in the morning. I walked towards my bathroom and took a long, relaxing shower. I thought it was supposed to soothe me, which it did, but my headache got a lot worse.

I put on my underwear, got dressed into a Batman t-shirt, and put on some black leggings. The perfect outfit for your bad days. I walked out of the bathroom once I was done, then I glanced at the window, and saw the boy next door having visitors. They were guys from my school, and all of them were people I knew. As soon as Kai glanced in my direction, I looked away and went to my computer.

I sat down at my desk with the window open next to me, the fresh air cooling me down. I messaged my friends on Facebook, checked out my other social medias, and watched a couple of videos I was tagged in. A while later, I noticed that the music died down, but my head was still killing me. I rubbed my temples before leaving my room.

Downstairs, I heard other boys talking. They were loud, and as I passed the living room, it looked like Connor was also having the guys over. They were arguing, and Matt seemed to be in the centre of it.

There was a lot of yelling, and I meant a *lot*. Most of the words were not even real words, just a bunch of noises that drowned in the echo of each other. It was a mess, so I decided to take matters into my own hands. I put my fingers to my lips and whistled so loudly, my ears might as well have bled from the noise.

Everybody fell silent and looked at me, but I was too hungover to deal with it. "Keep it down, idiots."

My voice was gone. It was barely just a whisper. It looked like I sang louder than I had originally meant to last night because all that was left was a raspy sound coming from my throat. I passed the living room and went to the kitchen where I poured myself a glass of water.

"Yo, Astrid. You okay?" It was Beck. He chuckled as he sat down on the stool next to the island counter. The guys all walked into the kitchen-slash-dining-room after me because they were both connected. I was the only girl in the house surrounded by boys who used to torment me.

"Peachy," I said with the power of sarcasm back in my hands. I missed it too. I searched through the kitchen drawers, trying to find some aspirin when I came up empty.

"Connor, do we have any aspirin? My head's going to explode," I said to him.

"Nope, Mom doesn't want us taking pills anymore, remember?" Everybody looked at my brother as he said that. "It's a long story, and it has to do with her being a nurse and all. She saw a lot of people get addicted, and now, she thinks that if it can't be dealt with time, you go to the doctor and let him decide. No self-medication," Connor explained to his friends.

"Ugh, don't remind me." I put my head into my hands. "I'm never, *ever* going to drink again. *Ever.*"

"Do you even remember what you did yesterday?" Beck asked, and I shook my head. I didn't remember much.

"No, and neither do I want to know, so keep it to yourselves," I ordered them.

"It's a shame because it's the first time in your life you actually did something interesting," Matt said. "And now you want to quit. I don't even know why I'm surprised."

"Just because your definition of interesting isn't the same as mine, it doesn't mean that mine matters less than yours," I replied, and I wanted to say something else until Connor interrupted me.

"Who's Luke?"

I froze. "What?"

"You and Adelaide talked about Luke. Who is he?" Connor asked.

"No one. Just an old friend. You don't know him," I said quickly and drank another glass of water, wishing it would be alcohol once more.

"Liar." Matt chuckled.

"It's none of your business, Matt, so stay out of it," I ordered before turning to Connor. "You too. Now, I'm going to call the girls and ask if any of them have some aspirin."

I picked up the house phone and dialled Diana's number. Addie slept over at her house. Most people knew my friends preferred each other over me, but I didn't really care, and I couldn't be surprised. My reputation ruined theirs, and every time we hung out, they got less popular.

I didn't even know how I got so hated. It was at the time when my best friend died, and I shut everybody out. I had so many friends I stopped talking to that started to resent and hate me. I said so many things to my brother when I was so struck with grief that my parents wanted me to see someone about it. Then my brother told *everybody* that our parents wanted me to see a shrink, which, of course, ruined our relationship once I found out. He stabbed me in the back. He betrayed me. Now, everybody liked him and felt sorry that he had a *crazy* sister.

I locked myself even more in that anti-social, loner bubble and didn't let anyone help me because I knew the only person who could help was me. Yet I didn't want to let go of that grief yet since she would be forgotten if I did. I didn't want her to be forgotten. Ever.

With the phone in hand, I stepped out on the front porch to have a private conversation. A couple of rings later, Diana finally picked up her phone. When I finished our conversation, I went back to the kitchen where I found everybody staring at me. "Addie and Diana will be here soon. I'll be in my room."

I walked up the stairs, and as soon as I entered my room, I felt chills go down my spine. When I closed the door and went toward my bed, hands wrapped around my body, one hand over my mouth to prevent me from screaming.

Oh my God, what should I do? I thought. I panicked, and me being me, I did the only thing that came to mind. I bit down the hand, hard. The attacker seemed taken aback, and I used this opportunity to grab his hand, twist it, trip him, and push him to the ground so that I was on top of him and he was lying on his stomach.

"Ow," I heard the guy groan in pain. His voice was one I knew. I let go of him, and he rolled around, with me still on top of him.

"Kai?" I asked, almost panicked, and felt anger seep through me. "What the hell are you doing here? You almost gave me a heart attack!" I slapped him over his chest and heard the laughter of many guys. When I looked up, I saw my window open. That must've been how he got in, but that's not what disturbed me.

His friends were watching us from his room, laughing their asses off. From the guys, I noticed there was Shaun Terrace, the school's sweetheart; JJ Walker, the prankster; Hunter Riley, one of the bad boys although nowhere as bad as Kai; Derek Peterson, the skater boy; Chester Kane, the boxer; and Mason Zachary from the football team. Never before have had I noticed that they hung out.

"As much as I would love to stay in the position we're in right now, my friends are going to get some crazy ideas," Kai smirked, and I got off him immediately. "How did you learn to do that? And by the way, what happened to your voice?" he asked after he stood up. I chose to answer only the first question.

"You pick up a few things if you have a brother whose best friend is the biggest asshat in the world." I managed to say and paused. "Well, almost." My eyes met his, and he chuckled.

"You better have a good explanation why you broke into my room," I demanded. He sent me one of his smirks again and turned around to look at my room.

"I don't know about that," he said, leaving me wondering. "Maybe I just wanted to see you."

He turned around, and his sentence actually made me roll my eyes. Not because it didn't make me feel all warm and fuzzy inside but because he was lying. Someone like him could never be with someone like me. We were very different.

"You know what? I really don't feel like dealing with you right now. Just get out." I pointed to the window. My head throbbed, and my throat hurt. Everyone was still laughing from Kai's room. He was halfway out the window when the door to my room opened.

"Just know that if you weren't our best friend, we wouldn't bring you any aspirin, but because you are, we can't let you suffer. Also, guess wha—" Diana stopped abruptly halfway down the path, causing Addie to bump into her back.

"Whoa, Diana, why did you stop?" Addie said as she side-stepped Diana and saw the scene in front of her.

"Uh, Astrid, you may not know this, but Kai is hanging out of your window," Diana told me.

"I hope he falls," I said, still a little angry at him for breaking into my room like a creep.

"I heard that," Kai said with a smirk plastered on his lips. "Girls." He winked at my friends right before he jumped onto the tree and climbed to his bedroom window. I threw myself on the bed and slipped under the covers. Diana rushed to close the window as Addie brought me a glass of water and an aspirin.

Addie put on our *Sick Days* CD. First song that came playing through my wall-mounted speakers was The Funeral by Band of Horses. Addie put me up to date on what happened after the party since Diana was too drunk to remember a thing.

They left the party at around three-thirty in the morning. She and Reese spent time together—and I didn't really want her to go into details—before she and Diana dropped Reese off. Addie drove to Diana's to sleep over and take care of her. Diana was sick, so they spent the whole night up in the bathroom, Diana puking and Addie holding her hair back. So here we were, all sick. Some more, some less.

I invited them under the covers, and we all ended up having an Iron Man movie marathon until the girls had to leave. Adelaide had a family dinner, and Diana had to drive her before going on a date with a guy she met at a party.

And that's what brought me to now, alone on a Saturday night. I took another soothing shower, happy that my head stopped aching. My throat was still a bit sore, though, and my voice was quite raspy.

I got dressed before coming to my room, ignoring the boys hanging out in Kai's room. I turned on my bed lamp. I decided to get some reading done since I'd been procrastinating for a while. I couldn't focus, as you might have imagined. With the boys downstairs and the boys at the neighbour's house, there was noise everywhere.

A while later, I heard my mom's car pull into the driveway, and I jumped from my bed, stormed down the stairs, and ran to the door. I slammed into her and wrapped my arms around her, which surprised my mom, but I didn't care. Saturday was the only night Mom came home early, and Sunday was the only night Dad did. I missed my parents. Call me a daddy's girl, but I got excited every time I spent some time with him.

"Hi, honey," Mom said, giggling as I hugged her before planting a big kiss on my forehead.

"Welcome home." I gave her a tight squeeze, then let her go.

"Good girl." Matt faked a cough behind me, and the guys laughed. I shot him a death glare when I noticed him checking me out. He sent me a wink, and I actually got the courage to flip him off.

Following Mom into the kitchen, I plopped down on the stool behind the counter as I watched her put some groceries away.

"So I talked to the Ashers today. I met them at the hospital," Mom said and bit her lip. Hospital? Why would Kai's parents be at the hospital? Wait, was Kai with them? "They're our new neighbours." Mom explained due to my silence.

"Oh, yeah? What did you talk about?" I asked, faking interest, knowing Mom wouldn't bring a story up unless she had something to say.

"Well," she said, tucking a strand of her hair behind her ear. "I took tomorrow night off so we could have dinner with them and get to know them better. They were originally meant to come over today, but we rescheduled."

I could hear how desperate she was to make a friend. Mom didn't have many friends because she had to work all the time. I think she saw this as an opportunity to make new friends, and it would be handy because they also lived next door.

"Why would you do that?" Connor asked, his voice snapping me right out of my thoughts.

"I don't know. They seemed nice, and they have a son your age. I thought you could be friends," Mom looked at me, and I knew what she was insinuating.

"Are you crazy?" I asked Mom. Me and Kai, friends? Okay, not that there was anything wrong with that, but I remembered listening to her lecture about not hanging out with people with a bad reputation and saying boy and girl friendships didn't work. She lectured me about safe sex and the risks of hanging out with guys. And now, suddenly, she was standing there in the middle of our kitchen saying just the opposite of what she taught me.

"That's no way to talk to me, young lady," she said in a serious voice.

"Right. Let me rephrase that. Are you mentally unstable and in need of a psychiatrist?"

"Astrid!" She started laughing and shaking her head at me.

"Mom, it's not like they're new to town. Their son is playing on the team." Connor came to my rescue. He seemed pissed off for some unknown reason.

"They're not? Oh, I didn't know." She thought about something for a few moments before she spoke again. "Still, they're your new neighbours, and I think it would be nice if we had dinner together."

Mom was naïve to think this dinner was going to be anything but a disaster. Connor and I shared a look, and instantly, I knew this was something we both agreed on.

Chapter 12

Dear Diary,

Due to the weird turn of events, there I was sitting on a Sunday night having dinner with Kai and his folks.

To my surprise, it went way better than I expected. Kai, Connor, and I stayed quiet most of the time as the elderly talked. By elderly, I meant our parents. Kai's parents were super nice. Mrs. Asher was so unlike anything I expected. She often talked about Kai and his childhood memories, making me wonder how he turned from that innocent little boy to who he was today.

I saw him squirm out of her hug, and it was obvious by the looks of it that he thought she was embarrassing him. Mr. Asher was okay too. He liked to talk about football, and he was a sports fan. Kai's father worked for a sports magazine and was used to wearing suits since he was the main editor. Kai's little sister Hannah was in the hospital because she caught some weird flu that had been going around middle school. That's why she couldn't make it, but Mr. and Mrs. Asher said she's getting out on Tuesday, so they were staying optimistic.

It got me thinking about my last few visits in the hospital. My heart ached at the thought, and my brain immediately shut down. I refused to think about it. Sometimes, it just got too much to handle.

Putting the fork down, I looked at my hands placed on my lap. I was distracted throughout dinner, but the parentals thankfully hadn't noticed. They were busy talking about work and even football. As you might have imagined, Connor and Kai were not even a little hesitant before joining the conversation. Not me, though. I stayed quiet until Mom called on me.

"Honey, are you okay?" She asked me, worry plastered on her fragile face. My mom looked quite like me when she was worried. Her eyes seemed sad, but her lips always tried to send a convincing smile that said everything would be alright.

"Astrid," my dad called my name.

"Huh, what?" I asked. *Damn, looks like I zoned out again,* my mind thought.

"Are you okay? You've been awfully quiet today. Something happened in school?" Mom asked.

I shook my head, not meaning to speak, but my lips didn't listen. "It's been a tough week. That's all."

I stood up and grabbed my plate. I felt a bit of anxiety around everyone in the dining room. I wasn't uncomfortable, but I was not comfortable either. Sighing, I put the plate in the sink and started washing it, but then I got company.

"You look cute when you're doing chores. In fact, I have a couple of things in mind you could do," said a familiar voice behind me, and I didn't have to turn around to see who it was.

"Keep wishing, neighbour," I said to Kai.

"Oh, I do keep wishing, but so far, my wishes hadn't come true," Kai replied. I snorted a very unladylike snort and turned around to grab the plate from his hands to wash it.

"Need help?" he asked.

"I've got everything under control," I responded. When I was finished, I dried my hands with a towel.

"You're not the control freak type, are you?" He teased me. His smirk was spreading as he leaned on the counter in front of me, his lean muscles visible under his shirt.

"I have a question," I said to him, ignoring his comment.

"Anything for you, love." He winked. *As if,* my mind screeched.

"How does your head fit into that shirt?" I said without thinking.

Kai looked taken aback. "Did you just say my head is big?"

"Certainly not as big as your ego," I retorted.

"Alright, lovebirds, settle down." Connor walked into the room, trying to bite back his laughter but was failing miserably.

"What? Me?" I pointed to myself. "Him?" I pointed to Kai. "Nuh-uh. Never. Gonna. Happen."

Okay, maybe that was kind of harsh. I wouldn't exactly say never when I thought about his abs whenever Kai's name slipped into conversation. *Never* was a strong word, but then again, so was *chemistry*.

Chemistry should be strong, and for two people to date, they had to have it, which Kai and I didn't have. He was just as arrogant to me as he was to other girls. He treated me like one of his toys just like he did with that girl on Friday's game.

"You know you love me," Kai said with a smirk.

"Kai, we're leaving!" his mom yelled, calling him.

"Leave." I snapped at Kai, pointing in the direction of the door.

"Geez, feels like marriage already," he muttered before giving me one final wink and disappearing through the door.

My face turned red at his remark, not because I was embarrassed, but because of anger. I turned to Connor who, by now, was in full spasms of laughter.

"Don't put ideas like this into his head!" I said, smacking the top of Connor's head.

"Do you have any idea how amusing your bickering is? Besides, I know nothing's going to come out of it anyway," Connor confessed.

"And how do you know that?" My anger was replaced by curiosity as I crossed my arms in front of my chest. I raised an eyebrow expectantly.

"Because I know *you*. You're very reserved. You mind your own business, and you don't pay attention to guys. You don't even pay attention to what's going on around you." Connor seemed to scold me.

"Hey! What's that supposed to mean?" I scowled.

"Well, you still haven't noticed a few of my friends have a crush on you. One of them since the first year of high school." Connor left the room before I could question him further. Me being me, I hurried behind him and followed him into his room. My brother wanted to protest, but I cut him off.

"You honestly didn't expect me to let you walk out of the kitchen without an explanation, did you?" A silence followed. "Oh my God, you did! So typical of you."

Connor was usually like this. He liked to tease me and torture me with his pranks. He also liked to know things I didn't.

"Well, I've already told you too much," he said, plopping down on his bed. I sat down in his chair while I looked around his room. It was a mess. The walls were painted dark blue, and there were clothes lying everywhere. He had a couple of posters taped on the wall featuring his favourite bands and a couple of football players.

"You weren't supposed to know, and if the guys find out, they're going to kill me." He groaned.

"I won't tell them. They won't even know I know, I promise." Connor's head snapped up to take a look at me. Normally, I would do anything to sell him out. It's just the kind of relationship we had. He was a pain in my ass, and my bite was just as dangerous as my bark.

Connor seemed to consider it for a few seconds, and then he sighed. "Nathaniel is the only one that doesn't like you that way. In fact, he keeps acting like your older brother and wouldn't stop defending you."

"You should take notes," I said in all seriousness.

"Stop with the sass, Sis." He rolled his eyes and cleared his throat. "I guess he feels protective ever since...you know, it happened."

I knew immediately what he was talking about. When Vanessa was in a coma, Nathaniel started talking to me. He came by to check on me every single day for over half a year to make sure I was okay—to make sure nothing happened to me. He was the only person who stayed by my side while Diana and Adelaide excluded me, saying they didn't need my drama in their lives.

They did that even though Vanessa was their best friend too. I was angry at them still, but I learned to live with it. I didn't know better. That's why I still remained friends with them. Nobody wanted to talk to me. I had no better option except being alone all my life. I lost Vanessa, and being alone just didn't feel like something I could survive. That kind of strength was beyond me.

That was when I thought about all the nights Nathaniel stayed up late talking to me over the phone even if I didn't say anything. He would ramble on and on, distracting me from the pain. Or when he, Matt, and Beck visited Connor and had a sleepover, Nathaniel would stay with me for a couple of hours, constantly asking if I needed anything. I always refused, though.

"Beck started liking you when we entered high school. I've seen him sometimes look at you differently, or he would start asking things about you. You were so caught up in grief that you wouldn't even talk to me for weeks." Connor took a deep breath before continuing. "Anyways, he confessed it to all of us when I wouldn't let it slip. It weirds me out that my best friend has a crush on you, but hey, at least I know he's a good guy. You could've ended up far worse."

I think he meant Kai, but I didn't say it.

"Matt and I were always closer and bonded more than I did with the other two, but I started noticing things after you came home from your vacation in California. You've changed so much after not seeing you those two months."

I remembered the looks everyone gave me. Mom gave me a ride home right before going back to work. The guys were home alone, swimming in the backyard and messing with each other. I was wearing a blue summer dress, and my hair was up in a high ponytail. It was a change from my normal sweats and baggy t-shirt that I wore before I left.

My closest friend from California, Jessie Samson was her name, decided I needed to dress up since I had to say goodbye to Luke. He was just a summer fling that I didn't tell anyone about. We didn't kiss, but we did flirt a lot and spend quite some time together.

I came home all dressed up and went to say hello to the guys. Connor immediately made some weird comment on how different I looked.

"Thanks...I think" was my reply.

"I didn't think the day would come when you didn't look like a twelve-year-old." Matt greeted me with his stupid remark. *I wanted to flip him off, but I didn't.*

I just took a deep breath and said, "As annoying as ever, I see."

"You look hot," Beck said. I rolled my eyes and laughed, not knowing how to react. I rarely got complimented by the guys. Nathaniel agreed with him, and when I was finished with greetings, I went back into the house.

Still, Matt's comment was something that caught my attention only now when I didn't seem to think twice about it back then.

"One night after you came back, the guys and I had our usual bonding night. We talked when he suddenly blurted out that he thinks he likes you."

Chapter 13

Dear Diary,

Today, Kai and I were supposed to study biology with the exam coming up in two weeks. He needed all the help he could get, but when he came over in all his glory, I knew we wouldn't get any studying done. In fact, he seemed to be more interested in my room. Right away, he walked toward my bookshelves and checked out all the books that were there. Needless to say, I was running out of space.

No matter what I did, I couldn't get him to concentrate on anything I was saying, as he kept staring at what my bookshelves had to offer. I was in the middle of telling him about cells when he interrupted me.

"I bet you wake up earlier in the morning than you have to just because you need to decide which book you're going to take to school," he said out of nowhere, and I was dumbfounded.

What came out of his mouth was true. Oh, the struggle I had to go through picking what to read. Ugh.

"Well, I bet you have problems when deciding which book to start next," I said back, and that seemed to turn into some kind of a competition which made him smirk.

"I bet you fall in love with fictional characters," he replied.

"I bet you cry over fictional characters," I shot back. He stepped closer to me, his eyes full of amusement before he said the next sentence very slowly.

"I bet you get so emotionally attached to fictional characters that you daydream about them whenever you get some free time."

"Only about boys," I admitted without thinking. Kai looked as if he won, but his eyebrow was raised, and he seemed to be amused. "What? Boys are better in books."

"Not better than me." He was dangerously close as we were staring each other down. He knew me just because he knew himself. In a way, that seemed to not only scare me but thrill me.

I never had anyone who could relate and knows what the struggle felt like. Then there was him—so alien yet so alike. Time seemed to stop when I was around him. He was not like anything I knew. He was a mystery to me, and spending time with him was something that I would always look forward to whether I liked to admit it or not. It was the truth.

He leaned forward, but before we could do anything else, my phone rang. He stepped away, clearing his throat, and I grabbed my phone from the desk. Connor's name was written on the screen.

"What do you want, Connor?" I asked, a bit annoyed.

"I'm at Starbucks. You want anything?" He offered, which was new. Too distracted to even hear what my brother was saying, I said the first thing that would get him off my back.

"No, thanks."

"Okay. I'll be home soon so I can take you book shopping since you've been nagging me about it for weeks."

"Did you say book shopping?" I asked, finally paying attention. Kai's head snapped up.

"Yup," my brother replied, and I had a feeling he was annoyed by now. I suddenly got an idea.

"Hey, can I call you back in a minute?" I asked him but didn't wait for an answer before I hung up. Then I turned to face Kai.

"Connor's taking me book shopping. Want to come?"

"Princess, you know that stepping into a bookstore can ruin my reputation," he responded to my question.

"I thought bad boys weren't supposed to care about anything."

"We do care about our reputations," he pointed out again.

"Oh, don't be an Al," I said, referencing to the Divergent books I saw sitting on his bookshelf. Al was considered as the ultimate coward, but that was also debatable.

"Are you calling me a coward?" he asked incredulously.

"Maybe," I said. "But it's more like I'm challenging you to step out of your comfort zone."

"Well, Ms. Bailey. Your challenge is accepted."

And that's when Kai and I went to the bookstore together for the very first time.

"I don't know what to buy," I muttered as I passed the fourth aisle for the sixth time. I had so much money with me since I'd been saving it for a long, long time.

"How about *The 5th Wave?*" he asked.

"Aliens?" I raised an eyebrow.

"Hey, don't give me that look. I've seen you reading the Lux series. And if I remember right, Luxen are aliens. Besides, *The 5th Wave* is awesome."

"Yeah, aliens made of light, and who doesn't love a good bad-boy-neighbour-with-a-sexy-mojo kind of story?" I said. As soon as those words left my lips, I knew what he was thinking.

"Like our story?" Kai insinuated, definitely amused. Everything I said seemed to amuse him.

"There is no *our* story," I replied, and he wanted to say something, but then his eyes glanced behind me. His mouth turned up, and he reached for whatever he was seeing. When I finally got to look at what he picked out, I saw a book series called Hush, Hush in his hands.

"By the angel! I've been looking for this for ages!" I exclaimed. "I heard so many things about it."

"Yeah, I know. I've read your blog."

"My—my blog?" I stumbled. I was surprised he even paid attention to me, but reading my blog? Oh, wow.

"Yeah. It convinced me to read *Legend* by Marie Lu. It was more than a decent read," he said. I wanted to jump up and down of happiness, but I forced myself to stay calm.

"Um, wow" was all I said.

We spent an hour more in the bookstore. Connor started getting impatient, so I sent him to get Christmas presents for our parents. I ended up buying Hush, Hush series, *The Lunar Chronicles*, Shatter Me series, and because the movie would come out soon, *Fifty Shades of Grey*.

Kai gave me an amused look when I picked it up. He whispered in my ear, "You know, you don't have to read about sex. I could show you a couple of things myself." He winked, and I punched him playfully in the arm. I knew he didn't mean it seriously.

He was just teasing me like always. I had him quite figured out by now. My stomach, though, felt alive with butterflies.

"Behave," I replied, rolling my eyes, but I was smiling.

Today was a good day, I thought to myself as Kai, my brother, and I headed back home.

Chapter 14

What's up, Diary? How's it going?

Me? I've been better. Connor had his friends over again the today. We were school-free because our school celebrated the so-called Principal's Day, and all the teachers went on a field trip. My brother had a guys' sleepover, and he wanted to get rid of me by trying to get me out of the house. He insisted on me crashing over at Addie's or Diana's house, but I refused because of a big history exam I had coming up. School was more important to me than his stupid sleepover, but he still wouldn't leave me alone. He even made me call my friends, but luckily, they said they had some other plans.

Diana was away for the day—a road trip with her family that was supposed to count as a bonding experience. So crashing at her place was a definite no-no. When I called Addie, I heard her cousin Peyton in the background, the same cousin she detested and hated. It meant only one thing—a family reunion. Apparently, her aunt and uncle were going on a vacation, and they left Peyton to stay with Addie's family. I felt really bad for her, and I wanted to ask if she wanted to sleep over at my place, but I wasn't so sure Connor would be up for that. At least not today.

It was noon when I came to the kitchen and saw the chores my mom had written for us to do on Post-it notes hung up on the fridge. My parents were working today as well, but I hoped to see them soon.

Connor strode in, and since doing the laundry was one of my chores, I also had to do his.

"Do you have any dirty laundry?" I asked as I grabbed the now full garbage bag.

"In my room," my brother replied, searching for large bowls for all his snacks.

"Would you mind carrying it all to the washing machine?"

"Do it yourself," he said, and though I asked again, he seemed to ignore me. Grunting, I took out the garbage and went into his room. It was an *absolute* mess, and *he* wanted to have a sleepover. Yeah, right.

I started picking up all the dirty laundry (yuck) and gathering it into a basket. Once that was done, I made sure all the dirty clothes were in the washer—including mine—before starting it.

I was used to doing chores, and it felt good to be independent. Plus, I liked some order in the house, which clearly didn't matter to my brother.

I did all the other chores, and once I was satisfied with my work, I decided to go back to my room and take a shower because I needed one badly. I had no idea how my brother could live in that god-awful room. I would get nightmares from just having to read there.

Then I got ready for the day.

When I came out of the bathroom, I was shocked with the sight before me. My brother and his friends were waiting in my room, seeming to be bored.

"Finally," Connor said.

"Took you long enough," Matt added.

"It's my room, and I can do whatever I want," I snapped. "Speaking of which, out!" I shouted and pointed to the door. I still wanted to put my makeup on, then head to the grocery store, as it was on my list of chores.

"Whoa, Sis, calm down," Connor said as none of them made any effort to move a muscle.

"I have things to do, and you've wasted enough of my time today," I snapped. "Get out of my room this instant because I am not in the mood to play your little games of torture today."

"But we just want to talk," my brother said innocently.

"You hear yourselves talk every single day. Missing one won't kill you," I replied.

"No, but it may make me forget how awesome everything that comes out of my mouth is" was his response.

"What is it with you and your ego?"

"I'll answer that if you answer me what's with your bitchy attitude."

"I asked you to help me today, and you straight out refused. You have been nothing but an ass to me all my life, and now you expect me to suddenly be okay with it?"

"You've been okay with it so far," Matt replied, leaning back on my bed in ease as I sent him one of my coldest, meanest stares.

"Well, I've fucking had it with you treating me like trash. I get enough of that every single day at school from everyone." I felt my breath hitch, but I didn't give in. I refused to cry in front of them.

"Wait, what do you mean?" Beck stood up and straightened his back, fully paying attention now.

"It didn't matter before, so it doesn't matter now," I replied, running a hand through my hair before grabbing my brother by his arm and throwing him out. "Get out of my room. All of you."

"Astrid, wait!" Connor protested as I locked my bedroom door behind me once everybody was out. "Who's been giving you a hard time?"

"Go away!" I shouted through the door as I wiped a few of my escaped tears and took a deep, calming breath before putting on my makeup.

"We'll stay here as long as it takes," Connor shouted back.

"What? Is it Annoy Your Sister Day?" I sighed in frustration.

"Maybe, but since you're not leaving the house, we thought we could talk to you," he replied. I snorted.

"I think I'm good," I said and went to the bathroom to dry my hair fully. The guys kept shouting my name once they realized I wasn't listening to them and that I wasn't going to open up either.

I started to study for my history exam, but I remembered about having to go to the grocery store. Deciding it was something that could be done some other time, I sighed and began to feel a little hungry.

So I opened the door, meaning to go to the kitchen, when I saw them all sprawled on the floor in front of my bedroom door. Connor and Matt passed each other a small ball, clearly bored as hell.

My brother was the first one to stand up, and I groaned. They were serious when they said they could be there all day.

"Hey, Sis," he spoke.

"What do you want?" I was surprised by how strong my voice was.

"Oh, we just wanted to talk to you." Matt pushed inside, not joking around as he said it.

Beck sat on the floor next to Nathaniel, and Connor sat on the chair near my desk while I stood awkwardly on the threshold of my bathroom.

Before any of them could speak, my phone rang. I picked it up and laughed silently at the name written on it.

Your Favourite Bad Boy ;) was written on the screen. When we exchanged phones, I put my number in his under the name *Young Adult Book Princess*. I still smiled at the memory.

"Are you going to answer that or just keep smiling at the screen?" Matt said. I decided to ignore Kai and not pick up. That would give him something to think about. I bet no girl he had ever called hung up on him. Well, now that's something I would like to do in the future.

"I'll wait out until it stops ringing," I replied.

"Why don't you just pick up?" Nathaniel asked.

"What's the point?" I saw their confused faces and barely held back my smile.

"Anyway." Connor cleared his throat. "We're here because—"

"Who's giving you shit?" Nathaniel blurted out, ready to kick some ass.

I sighed in a mix of anger and frustration. "Just leave me alone. I don't want to talk about school, nor do I want to talk about my life. You've never been interested in it, ever. So stop acting like you suddenly care because you'd only be lying to me. That would be worse than anything you've ever done to me so far."

"We didn't mean to hurt you. We just like messing around with you. You have to know that, Sis."

"Right. Insulting me, telling me to get lost and stop wasting space really didn't mean to hurt me in any way. Really. That makes as much sense as putting a Band-Aid on a gunshot wound," I replied sarcastically.

"I never said all that," Connor replied.

"Yeah, you did. Repeatedly. More than once," I stated.

The guys just looked at me shocked, apparently unaware of their behaviour and their actions, but I didn't feel sorry for them. Without apologizing, he cleared his throat and asked awkwardly.

"So who's been giving you a hard time at school?"

"Everyone. Take a look around for a change. Pay attention. You'll be quick to learn," I said. "Now, can we please change the subject because it's my free day and I need to study? Plus, I'm hungry."

Instead of waiting for an answer, I walked out of my room and straight into the kitchen where I got myself some cereal.

"You still didn't tell us who's Luke," Matt stated as I ate.

"I told you already. He's not someone you know, and I don't feel like talking about him. It's none of your business, anyway," I responded.

"Do we need to give you the sex talk?" Beck smiled in amusement as I narrowed my eyes at him, hoping this was some kind of a joke. Otherwise, I was going to die of humiliation. The guys laughed at my expression.

"You're joking, right?" I still asked to confirm my suspicions and to feel better.

"What? You think you don't need it? Actually, it would be fun." Connor laughed at me still. I waited for his laughter to die down a little so he could continue. "You should've…seen your expression."

I was lucky to finish my cereal, and I put my bowl in the sink before turning towards the door. "Goodbye," I said.

"Wait, where do you think you're going?" Beck asked and beat me to the door. He closed it, so I was trapped.

"If this is some sick joke just so you could get me out of the house for the night, you've won," I snapped. The guys looked at each other.

"Huh, we haven't thought of that," Matt said, still looking at my annoying brother.

"Yeah, but giving my sister the sex talk would still be more fun." God, Connor still liked to torture me. I bet he didn't even think about how embarrassing should it be done to him. He didn't think like normal brothers should, I tell you.

"No, seriously. Cut it out. I don't want to hear it. I already had to hear it from Mom, and once was more than enough." I reminded Connor of the time when Mom sat me down, and Dad sat him down on the same night in two different rooms. I had died of embarrassment.

"Yeah, but we were barely fifteen." Connor protested.

"I don't care. I don't need to hear it." I snapped.

"Why not?" Matt asked. I stayed quiet, thinking about what I was going to say, but the guys took my silence as an entirely different thing.

"Unless…" Nathaniel started.

"You've already had sex?" muttered my brother.

Ladies and gentlemen, that was how I found myself in some deep, *deep* shit.

Chapter 15

I stood there, not knowing what to do, not knowing what to say, neither willing to confirm nor deny because both would be equally humiliating.

After Connor had yelled *that* sentence out, I froze. Four pairs of eyes were on me. Connor was mad. Nathaniel was surprised. Matt looked downright jealous, and Beck just looked bored. I guess he just didn't care as much as everybody else.

"Well?" Connor asked, urging me to answer his question.

"Well, what?" I played dumb.

"Answer my question!" Connor shouted.

"Um…What was the question?"

Connor went from mad to pissed in less than a second. I turned around and tried to walk away, but Connor grabbed my wrist.

"Don't you *dare* try to walk away from me."

"Why do you care?" I started to defend myself.

"You're my sister," he shot back.

"So? I don't tell *you* what to do."

Connor was silent, and if his stare could burn through anything, I would have a hole in my head by now. He wanted to say something, but Matt spoke up.

"Relax, Connor. She didn't say she did it. At least not in those exact words."

"That's because what I do and do not do is none of your business," I replied calmly.

"You're not helping, Astrid." Matt gave me an exasperated look.

I yanked my hand out of Connor's grip, grabbed my phone, and stormed out of the house, away from all of them. I didn't know where to go, so I just walked. Not long after I started walking, I heard footsteps behind me.

"Astrid, wait." I expected someone else but hearing his voice surprised me so much that I came to an abrupt stop. He almost slammed into me, but I didn't turn around because I was mad.

"What do you want?" I said, trying to breathe.

"Hey, are you okay?" Kai asked. "Astrid, look at me." I sighed and turned around, looking anywhere but into his eyes.

"Look at me," he said again, and I found myself unwillingly gazing into his beautiful, rich brown eyes.

"What happened?" he asked me. I shook my head, and he chuckled quietly. However, it wasn't one of his usual chuckles. It was one that made my heart ache.

"It doesn't matter. Connor's just being a jerk."

"What did he do?" Kai urged me, his hands clenched into fists.

"Please. I don't want to talk about his royal asshat-ness." I begged him quietly and put a hand on his arm. He didn't say a word about it. Instead, he changed the subject.

"Come on," he said, clasping my hand. "I'm taking you somewhere."

And I went without any objections.

We rode half an hour until we arrived at the local beach that was a great diving spot. I looked at Kai who was watching me intently.

Without a word, he grabbed my hand and led me to the edge of the cliff. We sat down and listened to the ocean waves. He didn't let go of my hand, and we were sitting there, talking about anything and everything until the sun started to set. When he spoke after one of the longest silences, I heard hurt in his voice for the first time.

"I started coming here after Hannah was diagnosed with cancer." I looked at him, but he didn't return the look. Instead, he kept looking at the ocean. I didn't say anything, not because I didn't want to, but because I didn't know what to say. So I stayed quiet.

I slid my hand towards him and intertwined our fingers. It was a gesture to show him I was there for him, and though we didn't know each other that well, he could rely on me. We kind of became friends...I think.

He gave me a sad kind of smile, but I squeezed even tighter. He seemed to recognize that as a sign before continuing with his story.

"We didn't know anything was wrong. Her behaviour changed, so Mom and Dad took her to the doctors one day, and it went all downhill from there. She's in the hospital right now, and they say she's not going to make it. My parents lied about the flu. They just didn't want you to give us looks of pity. That's the reason we moved, anyway."

I get it. It's like a flashback, and it was all coming back to me now. I hated those looks. My parents, my teachers, even the doctors gave me those looks. That was the reason I escaped to California in the first place. I couldn't take it anymore. It was unbearable.

"It doesn't get better, you know?" I looked at where he was gazing. I could still feel the confused look he was giving me, so I explained. "They say time heals everything, but it doesn't. It leaves you with the most painful of memories. You wish you could go back and change things, prevent them from happening, but you're powerless and useless in this world."

There was silence until I added, "I'm sorry. I know these words are probably the last thing you wanted to hear." He squeezed my hand and sighed. I leaned my head on his shoulder, still watching the sunset. "But you know what? Your sister still has a chance. No matter what the doctors say, you need to believe in miracles for them to come true."

"What happened?" he asked me quietly after a brief silence. I wasn't prepared to tell him or open up—to anyone, for that matter—but there was just something about him. The way he asked—something in the way he spoke said he wanted to protect me from the pain. That was what made me speak about it for the very first time since it happened.

"Vanessa." I sighed. "She was my best friend, my sister from another mother. No, she was more than that. We used to do everything together and became best friends before I met Addie and Diana. She was always so supportive and was such a sweetheart. She was sincere, honest, loyal, and kind. Everybody knew her as the golden girl. That was what made Connor fall in love with her in the first place. They dated for six months before she went to Hawaii with her parents. There was a plane crash, and her parents died on the spot, but she was left in a coma with the worst of burns. I visited her in the hospital for two weeks straight, barely leaving her. My mom had to drag me out of there kicking and screaming. I was afraid she would wake up and I wasn't there. I was afraid that she would have to deal with her grief alone," I said. "I still remember watching her through the window of the intensive care unit. I watched her chest rise and fall," I managed to get out before taking a deep breath. "I watched the machines breathe life into her. I also watched her die as her lungs gave out."

I felt my eyes tear up, but I would not allow myself to cry. Not again.

"It's funny because I thought we'd have so much time left together. We loved baking and singing. She would come over to my house almost every single day, saying she missed me. Which was funny because we were neighbours," I said to Kai.

"You mean..."

"You moved into her house, yes. She used to live there, and I hadn't stepped foot into that room for years—hadn't even dared thinking about it."

Kai became speechless, but I wasn't done with the confession.

"I am sometimes afraid that she's looking down at me from the other world, disappointed at what I became—how broken and shattered I feel. She wouldn't want this, I know that, but at the same time, I can't stop missing her."

Kai nodded in understanding as he slowly slid his arms around me and held me tight in his embrace. Today, he helped me make progress in my life. I never spoke about Vanessa out loud. He helped me open up for the first time, and I was beyond grateful.

So I swore to be there for him when it came to Hannah no matter what happens between us. At that moment, we were each other's support.

For he was mine, and I was his.

Chapter 16

Dear Diary,

I didn't normally confess things, so opening up to Kai was a major step I for me. Also, I didn't normally talk about Vanessa.

But after we both opened up, it seemed as if Kai and I had a secret truce between us. I wouldn't exactly say we became close friends, but I didn't dislike him as much as I did before. Sure, he was full of sexual innuendos, and he implied to do dirty things with me all the time, but I guess that's just how he was. I misjudged him, though.

The week went by very quickly, and so did the one after that, and the one after that. Soon, the winter break arrived, and I was absolutely exhausted. School was keeping me on my nerves with the exams coming up, and I didn't have time to worry about anything else. After the New Years, everyone would have to take exams.

I hadn't bothered to worry about Kai or anyone else besides my girls. We studied in the library after school, or sometimes even at my, Diana's, or Addie's place. We were so consumed by it, knowing that we couldn't fail. Each one of us had different reasons.

Unlike Diana or Addie, I just wanted to pass the tests because I didn't want to fail. I hated failing as much as I hated beans. Not kidding.

So that was how I found myself studying in my living room couch, alone on Christmas Eve with Connor at some party and my parents working. Di and Addie had their own families to hang out with, and mine was nowhere to be found.

Feeling tired of studying biology, I headed up to my room and dressed in a sweater that had three words written on it: *Ugly Christmas Sweater*. I felt funky in my matching knee-high Christmas socks and some cute shorts. My house was relatively warm for this time of year, but seeing it almost empty made me sad.

I was singing along to Ariana Grande's Christmas songs when I got a text from Kai.

There's something in your room that you would want to read. Hint: it's in a place you store things.

I was confused as to what he could possibly mean, and I kind of got disturbed by the fact that he was in my room without me knowing. So I went through my closet because that was the first place I could think of. No luck.

Having trouble? he texted me. *When you find it and read it, give me a call.*

I looked around my room for a bit, thinking of how stupid I must have looked right now. My eyes landed on the drawers at my desk where I found an envelope addressed to me. I read the content of the envelope, admiring the neat handwriting. It said:

Astrid,

I wrote a message to you before but changed my mind seconds before you came through the door and kicked my ass. The guys are still giving me a hard time about it, btw.

All this time, I knew who you were. I knew you were Connor's sister who lost her best friend and the only girl in our school who chose not to butt into any of the chick fights. Connor often talked about you, threatening us to leave you alone. I didn't know why, but he seemed very serious and so did his friends. But you caught my attention recently, and I'll be honest that you were nothing like I expected.

I asked around about you because I was intrigued, and the more I learned from people, the more you surprised me. Their idea of you is completely wrong. You are not the shy, misanthropic girl everyone believes you to be. Sure, you came across as hostile when we met, but you had good reasons.

So I have to admit, the more time we spend together, the more I'm determined to get to know you better. So now, on Christmas Eve, I'm asking you this:

Just give me a chance and spend the rest of the day with me.

I put the letter down, unable to understand every single thought that went through my mind. Deciding not to overthink, I picked up my phone and called Kai. He hung up, not even answering, and before I could do anything, I heard a knock on my window.

Kai climbed the tree between our bedrooms so he could get to my room. I opened the window, still shocked by his sudden appearance.

"So, are you brave enough?" he asked, and I met his intense gaze. Kai's mouth wasn't shaped into a smirk. Instead, there was a small smile playing on his lips, and it was the first genuine smile I'd gotten from him.

He swaggered across the room and sat down on my bed. I couldn't help but admire his handsome features, the way his sharp cheekbones stood out and the intensity by which his jawline became even more visible. Some kind of emotion passed through him as I eyed him, and he did the same to me. My breath almost caught in my throat. *Was he checking me out?* I thought to myself.

"How long have you been waiting?" My voice was surprisingly steady.

"Long enough." His smile faded a little, but there was amusement hidden in his eyes.

"How many times have you done this?" I asked, meaning how many times he sneaked into my room.

"I don't know what you mean." He played dumb. He walked over to where I was standing with such ease. I couldn't believe my eyes. His face was inches from mine, and I had to look up because he was so tall.

"You know very well what I mean," I said bluntly.

"A couple," he answered my question, a smile again on his lips. It was a playful one—a smile I found I wanted to see more often.

"You do realize this makes you look like a stalker, right? Like Edward Cullen on a whole new level." I breathed out, not taking my eyes off him.

"I don't care," he replied, his gaze getting more intense by the second. A silence followed, and I couldn't find my voice. "Besides, Edward Cullen isn't so bad. He got what he wanted in the end." He pushed a strand of hair behind my ear. "So, are you done interrogating me?" he asked and took a step back, breaking the silence and this weird connection going on between us.

"No," I responded flatly, making Kai chuckle.

"Stop asking so many questions. Stop worrying and just trust me." He turned around and opened the door to my room.

"It's hard to trust you when you're so mysterious." I released a breath I didn't know I was holding.

"Most girls find mysterious guys sexy," Kai smirked at me.

"I like to think I'm unique," I shouted after I went into the bathroom to change.

"You certainly are," he said back through the door. When I came out, Kai offered me a hand, guiding me through the hallway. "Come on."

Why did I always blindly trust him? Why did I follow him anywhere he took me? The reason for this madness still eluded me.

Kai drove us to a cute little diner that was decorated with lovely Christmas decorations. Christmas lights were hung up everywhere. Not to mention it smelled like muffins, and I *adored* muffins.

The moment I set foot in this diner, I felt at home. I had never felt so comfortable at a place I'd never been to before, and I appreciated Kai dragging me out of the house. I would rather spend Christmas with someone I disliked or barely knew in a place I found I loved than spend it home alone. Which made me wonder...

"Why are you not home with your family?" I asked Kai as we sat down at the table. The normal lights were turned off, so we were left in the light of Christmas decorations, spreading more and more Christmas spirit.

"Mom, Dad, and Hannah went to visit Mom's parents while Hannah was still doing fine, but I wanted to pass," he told me.

"Why?" I asked, confused as to why he wanted to pass up especially if that might be his sister's last journey. Kai shrugged but explained further.

"I saw them during the summer when Mom and Dad sent me off to California to 'sober up,' and it didn't turn out so well. That's why I just told them to go while I watch over the house. I also might've used your family as an excuse," he implied and chuckled.

"Oh my God, what did you do?" I placed a hand over my face, pretending to be annoyed.

"I told them that I already made plans with you for Christmas. Which I did. You just didn't know about them yet."

I met his gaze and couldn't look away.

"But why would you want to spend Christmas with me? Don't you have a girlfriend to hang out with?"

"No. As a matter of fact, I don't."

"Right, because you're a bad-boy-wannabe and girlfriends would ruin your reputation," I said, half-joking, but the other half couldn't help but believe it was true.

"You're learning," Kai said, clearly impressed. Then he laughed softly and shook his head. "No, it's not that. I would have to give up girls, partying, and my freedom if I were in a relationship. Any potential girlfriend would have to be damn special if I was willing to abandon all that for her."

"So you go around and sleep with different girls every chance you get," I spoke. Kai gave me a weird and uncomfortable look, so I hurried up to explain. "I'm not judging you. I'm just trying to understand your ways."

"Enough about me. What about you?"

"There's nothing you don't already know. I'm hopelessly single, and I was about to spend my Christmas Eve alone, studying for my exams. Pitiful, I know."

"You lead an exciting life, Ms. Bailey. I would be honoured if you let me pick up a few things from you like your study habits. They fascinate me to no end. How on Earth can you study so much without your head bursting with all the knowledge?" He seemed to be genuinely intrigued, so I shrugged.

"Some are just born awesome," I replied but then sighed. "You'll get bored of me soon and move on with your girl toys."

"I beg to differ."

"You'll see," I said, and the waitress came to take our order. We talked about the Christmas party Connor was at, then school, then us.

"I can't believe you never tried Oreos," I exclaimed. Kai shrugged and smiled.

"I just thought the hype would ruin it for me. Everybody says how good they are, but if I tried them, I'm just afraid I'll be disappointed."

"I dare you to try them," I said.

"And what do I get if I don't like them?" Kai smirked.

"Um…" I thought about it for a few moments before coming up with an idea. "If you don't, then you'll owe me a favour."

"Why do I have to owe you a favour? Why don't you owe me one?"

"Because if you won't like them, then you have to be punished."

"I like the sound of that." Kai wiggled his eyebrows, and I hit his shoulder playfully. "But what if I do like them?" Kai crossed his arms over his chest, making his muscles stand out.

"If you do, then I owe you something. For trying them, of course."

"Okay, it's a deal, baby doll."

An hour and a half later, Kai and I were sitting on my porch, me watching the stars and Kai starting to open a box of Oreos. I eyed the box hungrily, barely holding myself back from taking it off his hands.

"You ready?" he said, and I turned to him. His eyes were intense again, and my eyes slipped to his lips for a moment before looking back up. I nodded slowly and smiled teasingly. He opened the box and put an Oreo cookie between his pearly white teeth, taking his time.

He bit into it, and I spent the next few seconds on edge. Kai's expression was carefully guarded.

"So? What do you think? Say something already!" I smacked his arm.

"Ow," Kai muttered as I stared him down in annoyance. Slowly, his lips turned into a smile.

"I'm thinking about cashing in a favour you owe me," Kai said. I was ecstatic.

"You like them?" I asked happily. He nodded, and I smiled and hugged him. Then when I pulled away, I remembered his words. "Wait, what kind of favour?"

Kai's eyes stared at my lips, and he said in a low voice two words I least expected to hear.

"Kiss me."

And that, dear Diary, was just the first epic turn of events that happened on Christmas.

Chapter 17

I took in a sharp breath that echoed in the silence now spreading between us.

"What?" I asked Kai, my voice as soft as a whisper.

"A kiss. That's how I want to spend my favour."

"I…I can't," I said to him.

"You can if you want to," he said to me. He leaned his forehead into mine. Our noses were touching, and our lips were centimetres apart. He was so close, and I was so tempted to do it.

"Fine," I said, leaning in to kiss his cheek. His skin was soft, and he actually chuckled as I did so.

"What was that?" he asked when I pulled back.

"A kiss," I replied innocently.

"That was definitely not a kiss." Kai laughed.

"Well, you didn't specify what kind of a kiss you wanted."

Kai was now in fits of laughter, and I smiled because I loved his rich laugh. "You're so out of this world, I swear," he spoke when he calmed down a bit.

"Is that a good thing?" I asked.

"The best," he replied with a smile as his hand brushed against my cheek. "But that was still cheating, and I can't let you get away with it. Luckily for you, I'm going to be merciful," Kai said teasingly. He was half smirking when I cut him off.

"If you're going to imply anything sexual right now, I'm going to hit you," I warned, which made him chuckle again.

"No, I wasn't going to imply anything sexual. I was going to invite you to the school's Winter Formal that's about to start in two hours. I have an extra ticket and no date."

I was dumbfounded.

"It's funny because only you would think I was going to imply anything sexual. Besides, you could owe me a thousand of favours, and I still would never make you do something you didn't want to do. Maybe it's because you've grown on me in the past two months."

"Oh" was all I managed to say. His words surprised me. Plus, I totally forgot about the formal. I already bought a dress in case I would go, but it didn't seem that important, so it slipped my mind. I guess I was just too damn busy with school stuff.

"I'll pick you up in an hour and forty-five minutes," he stated and tried to walk away.

"But I didn't even say yes," I said in protest.

"You owe me, princess." Kai turned around and winked at me.

"Damn it!" I pretended to be angry. He sent me a teasing smile, and I waved him off before going into my house and closing the door behind me. I leaned back and closed my eyes

*Kiss me...You've grown on me...*His words still echoed in my ears.

I smiled at myself, replaying those words in my head before I remembered that I had a dance to go to. I quickly ran up to my room, took my phone out, and texted Addie and Diana, telling them about my plans.

I made sure the curtains were closed so Kai couldn't see how I looked before he picked me up.

As I got ready, I couldn't help but feel more confident than insecure. It had been a long time since I felt that way, and I was glad for it. The dress I had picked out was a perfect fit that made me feel elegant. But I knew the dangers of going to the Winter Formal—the bullies and the angry cheerleaders.

My brother's friends and enemies were all the same to me. Both were ruthless, and both were cunning. I would normally be shaking before going to the formal, but I was going with Kai. I knew he wouldn't let anything happen to me.

Kai was at my door before I knew it. I grabbed my stuff and made sure I looked okay. I also sprayed just the right touch of my favourite perfume before opening the door.

My breath caught in my throat. He was wearing a tuxedo, looking as handsome as ever. His gaze was dark and sexy. He offered me his hand, and I nervously took it.

"You look so seductive," Kai said. "I'm beginning to think inviting you to the formal was a bad idea. I'd much rather be somewhere quieter now that I think of it."

I laughed when I would normally blush and look down. It felt good to be complimented in that way. It felt good to be desired even if it was from a guy who sleeps with every willing girl he met. "Your charm is irresistible, your highness," I said in sarcasm.

"Don't believe me?" Kai asked as he took a step towards me, cornering me against the wall. He had my arms pinned up. I was trapped, unable to move. His breath was on my neck. "You have no idea how beautiful you are. I have a hard time resisting doing anything stupid," he said, and I made myself stand still.

Then don't, my heart said, but my mind was telling me a whole different thing. Kai was a bad boy—*the* Bad Boy. Collecting hearts was what he did for fun, taking them to bed and then leaving them on the sidewalk.

Before I knew it, his hands were cupping my cheeks, and his eyes bore into mine. "You always look beautiful. Don't forget that. If anyone tells you otherwise, I'm going to make sure they never say anything like that to you again. You're worth more than you realize, Astrid."

I looked into his eyes, and I felt a sudden wave of desire. It was when he said things like this that my heart melted. He kept looking at me for a few moments before he took a step back. Then he offered me his arm, and I took it.

"Thanks," I whispered, a little flustered as I released a breath. I met his smile with my own.

Chapter 18

Kai drove in the new car he got as a present. His parents were happy to buy him one while mine weren't so lenient. They thought I was not yet ready to drive after the accident happened, and that was months ago. I was being treated as their little girl who went through a traumatic experience, and they were afraid I would have a mental breakdown once I sat behind the steering wheel again.

Luckily, Kai's parents weren't as overprotective as mine, so I got the honour of being the first person to ride with him in his new car.

When he parked the car in an already full parking lot, people started turning around, staring at us. I knew Kai looked extremely good, and that alone made lots of girls swoon, but when he opened my car door and helped me out, I was pleasantly surprised. The attention I got wasn't *that* negative. I saw some guys stare as if they hadn't recognized me.

I saw jaws drop and girls gasp. It was a bit overwhelming, but I got through it as Kai offered me his arm and whispered in my ear.

"I told you," he spoke in a comforting tone. "Are you ready to show who Astrid Bailey really is?"

"You already know," I replied.

"Not to me. Show *them* who the person they've been picking on all these years is. Show how fierce, incredible, and talented you are. Stop hiding behind your fears, Astrid. They'll catch up to you sooner or later."

"How do I show them all that by simply going to a formal?" I asked.

"Let go. Make this a night where you don't let your anxiety get to you. Hang out with someone other than Diana and Adelaide."

"I have a feeling you don't really like my friends," I said out loud.

"Honestly? I don't. Diana has a history with me—one that I do not want with her. She's been trying to get in my bed for ages, and no matter how many times I rejected her, she wouldn't give in."

"You rejected her?" I asked incredulously.

"Of course. I had to have some standards," he said as we passed some halls and waited in line to show our tickets. "But that's not the reason I dislike Diana or Adelaide for that matter. I've seen how they treated you, and I sometimes wonder why you're still friends with them."

"It's either them or face the whole school alone, Kai. It's not like I have a choice. Besides, they're really not that bad once you get to know them better. The only problem between us is that we don't really know each other anymore."

"To be frank, I'd rather be alone than have fake people in my life."

"That's you. You're loved by everyone and desired by almost every single girl. You are successful, funny, and popular. Me? I'm known as the school's loser who can't keep up with her brother.

I'm hated because I like to study and read books, and I get bullied on a daily basis. Just last week, a girl spilled her drink on me in the cafeteria because she thought I deserved it," I said. "You and I, Kai, are living in two different worlds, and we've been shaped into two different people. You're strong, and I'm not."

Kai looked at me and thought about what I said. "You're stronger than I am, Astrid. *You* are the one who's been going through this, not me. You have to give yourself more credit than that."

It was overwhelming, his belief in me. The way he saw me was so far from what I felt like, but it felt good to have someone believe in me for the first time in my life.

Before I could respond, it was our turn to show the tickets which Kai took out of his jacket. He handed them to Delilah who was in charge of letting people in.

Delilah was surprised to see Kai and me arm in arm, but the grin she gave me was one of happiness. She and I always got along extremely well, but she was surrounded by cheerleaders most of the time, so we didn't really hang out. A few of the cheerleaders often gave me a hard time, but Delilah was definitely not one of them.

When Kai and I stepped into the school gym, we saw our classmates dancing, and it looked fun. My eyes found Addie and Diana who turned to me with their mouths wide open. Kai looked at me and asked if I wanted something to drink. I said no, mentioning the last party and the promise I made to myself to stay away from alcohol. Of course, the school drinks were always spiked.

I asked Kai if he was going to drink, but he shook his head, saying that he didn't need alcohol to have fun. Anyways, he was going to be my ride home, and he didn't do drinking and driving.

"I like the way your mind works," I said to Kai, and he smiled.

"Want to head over to your friends?" he asked, and I didn't even have time to answer before he pulled me with him in their direction. Kai greeted Reese in a way guys greeted each other while Addie, Di, and I talked.

"You look beautiful," Diana said.

"Absolutely gorgeous," Addie agreed.

I blushed, then Reese turned to me. "Hi, Astrid. You look fantastic."

I heard Kai growl, "Don't flirt with my date, Harrington."

I giggled and elbowed him playfully. Kai's expression softened when he looked at me and winked. I liked this playful attitude. It was such a change from the first time we met. He wasn't as intimidating as I thought. Then again, I always tended to overreact. It was something I got from my parents.

Kai and Reese excused themselves and went to say hello to the other guys.

"So, you two seem to get more comfortable with each passing day," Addie said to me.

"It's not like that," I replied.

"Really? Because I got a text from one of the cheerleaders who was on her way to get ready for formal. She said she passed by your house and saw you kiss him."

"I didn't kiss Kai," I responded, but then I remembered. "Oh, wait."

"I knew it!" Diana exclaimed.

"But it was just a kiss on the cheek, nothing more."

"On the cheek? Astrid, if you're going to kiss a guy, do it *properly*." Diana scolded me.

"We're just friends, and I don't want that to change. I'm not prepared for anything serious, and to be honest, I'm sure he's not either. He's a bad boy for the love of Oreos."

"Right because he always invites the nerdiest girl in school to be his date to the dance. It's totally not unusual," Diana said sarcastically. "Especially when he always appears alone at every single party. It's not like you're special or anything."

I ignored her comment as they continued to interrogate me for a while before dragging me onto the dance floor. I tried to get as comfortable as I could with people watching, but not having alcohol to give me courage was hard. I knew I should let myself have fun; Kai wanted me to have fun. So I took a deep breath and tried to shut the world out when one of my favourite songs came on. It ended way too soon, and I felt an arm on my back. It was Beck's.

"Excuse me," he said to me. "May I have this dance?" He offered me a hand, and when I hesitated, he said, "Your date approves. I asked."

I looked at Kai who smiled and nodded. "Yes, you may," I said as he stepped in front of me, guiding me with his arm wrapped around my waist. We danced, not breaking eye contact, both of us smiling.

"I almost didn't recognize you. You look different. Good different," Beck said after a while. I blushed and looked away.

"Thank you," I said and looked at Addie. She smiled as she danced with Reese, her white dress flowing around her beautifully.

"I'm serious, though. I'm glad to see you're being more sociable," Beck said. "And I don't mean that as an insult. I just mean that after everything that happened, it seems you're finally starting to heal."

"I'm trying," I replied, a bit tense by the conversation topic. I didn't want to talk about her today. I didn't want to talk about her to anyone.

"I owe you an apology for letting Connor and Matt treat you like that. It never occurred to them or me that you might get hurt," he said.

"We got too used to the way things were that we stopped noticing them anymore. We make excuses, and we go our separate ways after that. It's always been like that, and neither of us can change it. So I don't need your apology."

We changed the conversation topic to something lighter before the song ended. My brother was by my side after that, asking if he could talk to me. He pulled me off the dance floor so we could speak in private.

"I need to ask you something," he said.

"What is it?" I was worried.

"Matt's having a party in an hour, and I need to know if you're going."

Right then, Kai appeared by my side. "Hey, dude," he said and gave my brother one of their bro handshakes.

"Hey, Kai. Wassup, man?" Connor smiled. I didn't know if he liked Kai or was just friendly, but he definitely didn't look happy when Kai drew an arm around my waist. In fact, he scowled.

"Nothing much, I was just looking for Astrid." He looked down and smiled. I felt slightly embarrassed about acting this way in front of Connor, and I had a feeling that Kai was doing this just to provoke him.

"So?" Connor asked impatiently. "You going?"

"Going where?" Kai asked.

"To Matt's party," I explained.

"You want to go?" Connor asked him.

"Only if Astrid wants to."

"I don't know," I said unsurely. "I mean, I guess we could stop by."

"Okay, great," Connor said and left before I could take another breath. It was clear he felt more than awkward standing there. Kai was looking at me weirdly, and he removed his arm from behind my waist.

"What?" I asked.

"Nothing. I'm in a bad mood. Let's just go," he said and grabbed my arm.

"We don't have to go to the party if you don't want to. We can just go home."

"It's fine, Astrid. I want you to go and have fun."

"Will you at least tell me what's wrong?" I asked, starting to become a bit worried.

"I don't feel like talking to you about this right now," he replied.

"Okay, as you wish," I said, feeling a sudden urge to roll my eyes. He built walls around himself to stop people from taking a look at who he really was, but his act didn't fool me. "Do you want me to give you some time to yourself? If you don't want me here, I can just go. We can meet at the party."

"I don't want to do that to you," he said.

"It's fine. I don't mind. I just want you to be okay."

I gave him my first ever hug, which surprised him, and he kissed my forehead. When I pulled back, I caught Matt's eye, and he was definitely not pleased with what he saw.

I searched for my friends after that but couldn't find them, so I headed over to my brother's friends—the company I didn't exactly like.

"Hey, guys, what's up?" I asked as I approached. Matt, Beck, and Nathaniel were standing there, talking to each other. I had no idea where my brother was, and I couldn't care less.

"Hi, Astrid! You look beautiful," Nathaniel said, and I gave him one of my charming smiles. The guys didn't have any girls hopping around them, but it didn't mean they were here alone. I still had to watch out because hanging out with them would make me the target for the night. Whether it was jealousy or just my brother's publicized dislike of me, I didn't know what pushed them to pick on someone they never even talked to.

"We thought you weren't coming to the Winter Formal," Matt said.

"Yeah, I wasn't planning on coming here either."

"Who are you here with?" Nathaniel asked.

"Kai," I replied. The look on Matt's face was of utter surprise.

"Anyways." I cleared my throat. "I don't want to ruin your guy time, so I'm just going to be quick and ask if anyone has seen Addie or Diana."

The guys shook their heads. "But you can stay here and hang out." Beck offered.

"Yeah, I don't think so."

"What? We're not good enough for you, sweetheart?" Matt said. Beck elbowed him.

"You tell me since you seem to be the expert."

Matt laughed bitterly then shook his head. "Forget it," Matt said but then seemed to change his mind. "Actually, you know what? The one time I try to be nice to you, you don't seem to appreciate it."

"You being nice to me? It was Beck who offered me to stay. The only thing you did was ask me a question, and that's it."

"When I normally would've insulted you by now," Matt defensively said.

"And why? Why on earth do you want to bring me down so badly?"

"Because it seems to be the only way to burst that little bubble of yours. You need to notice the outside world for once!" Matt snapped.

I let out a sigh and rubbed my temples. "You know what? I don't need this," I said and turned around without a word.

And they said women were frustrating.

Chapter 19

I found Adelaide in a fierce make-out session with Reese, so I turned around and pretended I didn't see anything. Diana was dancing on the dance floor with guys grinding behind her that she shooed away as soon as I came closer.

"Oh, baby girl, what's wrong?" she asked as she walked off the dance floor.

"Nothing." I smiled a fake smile.

"I know you're lying." She sent me one of her looks, and when I didn't tell her what happened, she continued. "Let's go to the restrooms."

She led the way, and by some miracle, the restroom was empty. There was nobody in the stalls, so Diana took the chance and locked the door. "Okay, spit it out," she said.

"I just…" I stammered. "It was the first time in weeks that I had the opportunity to have fun, and it started great. I just wish she could be here. That's all." I sighed, feeling so lame to be talking about her again, yet I couldn't help but miss her. She should've been here for this. We should've gone together to the formal.

"Oh, come here. Life goes on. The least you could do is enjoy it for her too." Diana pulled me into a hug.

"Now, this is what *you're* going to do. You're going to get out there." She made sure my hair looked perfect. "You're going to smile like you've never been happier." She put some nude lipstick on me. "You're going to show those beautiful grey eyes of yours, and you're going to blow them all away. You know why?" I shook my head. "Because you're Astrid Ella Bailey, and you're the strongest person I know."

That made me smile. As we walked out, I tried to breathe and tell myself they would forget about me and move on or that they were looking at Diana.

I hated the attention. I really did. I just tried to forget about it and fit in.

Some time had passed so Diana and I started looking for Addie. I noticed that none of the guys were here anymore. We found our best friend with Reese and asked if they were coming with us to the party. They both declined, and I started getting second thoughts about it.

"Oh no, you don't," Diana said, reading my mind. I put my hands up in defeat as she led me to the parking lot. I thought she was going to drive to Matt's house in her Mini Cooper she got as a gift when she got her license, but she stopped at my home first.

"Why are we here?" I asked.

"You, my darling, are going to change out of those clothes. They're too formal, and you don't want anyone spilling their drinks on that gorgeous dress."

Before I could protest, she grabbed a bag of clothes from the back seat and dragged me into my house. We spent yet another hour on my looks. I knew better than to protest. If I even tried to make her change her mind, she would've tied me down and undressed me herself. She was *that* into makeovers.

"There. You're done." She let me turn around and walk in front of a mirror. This dress wasn't as elegant as the other one, but it was a bit more daring.

"What do you think?" Diana asked.

"I think I'm falling in love with myself," I said, only half-joking. I had never felt this good in my life.

Every space around Matt's house was packed with cars. Every parking lot was full, and we barely found a place to park. Before Diana stopped the engine, she looked at her phone. "Fashionably late as ever." She gave me a mischievous grin before getting out of the car. We had to walk in high heels—something I loved doing and didn't care if it ruined all the nerd stereotypes. Stereotypes were overrated, anyway.

When we entered the house, twice as many people were there. There were red cups everywhere, and people were drinking, many of them making out. It was a complete mess.

"Who's ready to party?" Diana shouted, and people shouted back. My best friend muttered something about getting us drinks, and I requested Sprite.

People from my class started coming up to me and complimented me, saying I looked nice. I was pretty sure most of them were drunk or halfway there. I smiled politely and thanked them all while blushing like crazy. Nobody was ever this nice to me.

I felt somebody grab my hand for the hundredth time today, and I sighed.

"What?" I snapped when I saw who it was.

"Couldn't you wear a more revealing dress?" Connor said sarcastically. I punched his arm none too lightly.

"What I wear or do is my own business," I hissed.

Connor dragged me to his friends and a couple other football players all standing in a circle. I stood there, totally uncomfortable. I saw Matt walking to join us, but his name was called. He turned around and saw the one, the only...

Cindy.

I groaned in my mind. I really disliked her so, so much. She wore so much perfume, you could smell it from where I was standing.

"Babe, why aren't you spending time with me? We barely get to see each other," she said in her wanna-be-sweet voice. When she looked at me, she frowned.

"What is *that* doing here?"

"She is my sister, and unlike you, she's actually a decent human being, so you'll show some respect," Connor snapped at her.

"Whatever." Cindy flipped her hair and turned to Matt. "Come to bed with me. I'm lonely," she said.

"Uh, I don't know. Maybe later," Matt said and started to walk away. She had his arm, and he turned around annoyed.

"Come on. We could have a good time. You know..." she said, fixing his shirt. Someone coughed.

"Way to get manipulated by a woman," one of the jocks said. Others laughed. I saw that something wasn't right here. Something just didn't feel right. I mean, I knew Matt didn't really like her, but he was still a player, and he never turned his stupid ass girlfriend down. Why was he hesitating?

"You know what? Maybe some other time," he said to her and headed outside.

"There will be no other time!" she yelled behind him in her annoyingly high-pitched voice. Matt only waved her off, and I turned to see Diana coming where I was standing, carrying my drink.

I headed off to meet her halfway, as far away from that group as I could.

"Hey, what was that about?" she asked me. I shrugged because I didn't know.

She handed me my drink, and I felt slightly awkward. None of us talked because we didn't know what to say. So instead, I drank my Sprite.

"I think you should talk to him," she said.

"Why me?" I asked in surprise.

"Because you're Astrid Bailey, and you know how to get people to trust you...to talk to you. Besides, he has such a low opinion of you that in his mind, it would be like talking to thin air."

"Thanks, Diana. You make me feel so much better about myself."

"Well, it's the truth, isn't it?" she asked, and without responding, I turned around and headed outside. On the way, I had to step over somebody that was lying on the ground. I closed the door behind me and saw Matt sitting on the railing of his front porch.

He didn't hear me coming, which was weird since there was loud music playing and could be heard even louder when I opened the door.

"You okay?" I asked him and put my hand on his back. He seemed startled.

"I'm fine," he responded.

"It sure doesn't seem like it," I said. I hopped onto the railing. Matt was facing a different direction, facing the driveway, and I was facing toward his house. He met my stare with an unreadable expression.

"Why do you treat me nicely after I've been such a dick to you?" he asked.

I thought about it for a moment. "Maybe it's because I know what it's like not to have anybody to talk to. It sucks." A silence followed.

"You've always been too good to others," Matt muttered quietly, and I was sure he didn't want me to hear it. I ignored it and ruffled his hair instead.

"Come on, dork. There's no way I'll let you stay outside while there's a wild party raging inside your house," I exclaimed then somehow dragged him inside. Matt rolled his eyes and smiled. I felt a little better about it.

"I'm going to head to the kitchen to get a drink," he informed me.

"I'll go with you," I told him. He offered me his hand, and I took it.

When we entered the kitchen, what I saw did not only shock me. There was a part of me that felt hurt.

I saw Kai and Cindy in a passionate, half-naked make-out session.

Chapter 20

Dear Diary,

I let myself be vulnerable. I played with fire, and I got here. Some part deep down inside got attached to Kai and momentarily forgot what he was—or tried to think I was wrong.

As I stood there with Matt by my side, Kai pushed Cindy away without noticing us yet.

"What are you doing?" he asked her in disgust.

"Matt won't sleep with me, but I know you will," Cindy replied, twisting a strand of hair between her fingers.

"You're mad," he said to her as Matt cleared his throat rather too loudly. The two froze, and Kai looked at me instead of Matt.

"Astrid—" he spoke as Cindy covered herself as if *us* snooping around would be outrageous. She gave us dirty looks before walking out, head held high like nothing happened.

"Having fun?" I asked him, and he looked absolutely mortified.

"It's not what you think—"

"Why are you apologetic?" I asked. I wasn't his girlfriend, anyway. He was free to do whatever he wanted.

Matt couldn't even look at Kai. He only shook his head in disapproval and walked out of the kitchen. As soon as he was out, Kai walked closer to me, but I took a step back, feeling the proximity between us would be too much.

"She kissed me. You have to know that."

"Don't you get it, Kai? I'm not your girlfriend. You can do whatever you want. You don't need to justify your actions. It's not like I care, anyway." That was a low blow, but I forced myself not to care about it. He did push Cindy away, but just feeling what I did at that moment was shocking to me. I felt jealous.

"Okay. Then you wouldn't care if I slept with half the school?"

"You already did, didn't you?" I said, only half serious, and he whistled.

"Wow, you are feisty today, aren't you?" he asked, making me shrug. "Do you want to know what I think? You care more than you're willing to admit."

"Whatever, Kai. I have better things to do than be here talking about you sleeping with girls," I replied.

"You're hiding away from your feelings, Astrid. You're afraid."

"Stop trying to analyse me because it's not going to work," I said before Diana came into the kitchen.

"Do you want to sleep over tonight? We didn't do that in a long time," she offered, and I accepted. After that, I said goodbye to Kai, and we left the party.

When we arrived at her house, it was two in the morning, and it was pitch black. Diana parked the car, and I followed her to her room. We watched a movie, and I really didn't feel like talking as

Kai and Cindy's kiss kept replaying through my mind. I couldn't even concentrate on the screen in front of me. Tonight's event rushed through my head.

He was right. I did care. But why? Maybe because he was my neighbour, my classmate, and my friend?

In the morning, I woke up in Diana's bed. I heard my phone vibrate on the nightstand, so I swiped to unlock it and saw fifty-nine text messages and twenty-three missed calls. I saw Connor's name pop up, but then again, so did Matt's, Beck's, Nathaniel's, and Kai's. I had no idea what to make of it.

Diana stirred beside me, and I felt her wake up.

"Uh, what time is it?"

I glanced down at my phone and saw it was already two PM. We slept through the whole morning. The guys must've been freaking out.

"It's two PM. Come on. We overslept. Actually, that's an understatement. I need a drink, and we need to get some food into our system," I said, probably overreacting because I was used to waking up early.

She dragged herself out of the bed while I looked at myself over in the mirror. Damn, I was a mess.

I had black marks from mascara, my hair was worse than it was in the morning. I pulled my dress down and cleaned my face. I asked Diana for some comfy clothes and went to change.

Later, I walked down the steps, tying my hair into a ponytail. Diana and I ate in peace, and later, she took me to the barn to say hello to the horses. Diana's family had been raising horses and taking care of them for years.

Diana and I then went to the lake where we spent some time together when my phone vibrated again, and I remembered that I forgot to reply to all the text messages.

So I picked up the phone only to receive another call.

"Hello?" I said.

"Astrid! Oh, thank God! You had us worried sick! Where have you been? Why aren't you home? Everybody's freaking out!" Adelaide said, and I heard someone take the phone from her.

"Astrid?" Connor's voice came through the line. "Are you okay? Please, tell me you're okay." He sounded worried.

"Connor, I'm fine. I'm at Diana's. We've slept until two PM and then went to the lake."

"Do you have any idea how worried I was? You scared the living shit out of me! I wanted to call Mom and Dad—"

"Wait, they don't know, do they?" I asked him.

"No, but they'll be home in an hour, so you better get your ass down here and—"

I hung up. Diana and I got back to her house soon after that. She was going to drive me back home after I changed. I had the dress on and the heels again.

When I came home, I closed the door behind me and walked to the living room where I heard voices.

I saw Connor, Matt, Adelaide, Beck, and Nathaniel standing there, just looking like they hadn't slept in a long, long time.

Chapter 21

Everyone was gathered here and didn't even notice me until my phone rang. Then they all jumped up, clearly startled by my sudden arrival.

I looked down at my phone and saw Diana's number written on the screen. "Diana?" I answered. I looked at the familiar faces of Addie, my brother, and his friends that came into view.

"Astrid! Just wanted to tell you that I'm going to Italy tomorrow. My parents just told me that they're taking me to Europe!" she screamed excitedly.

"What?" I said, feeling happy for her but feeling sad at the same time because I assumed she would stay with me through the holidays. But still, I was happy for her.

"I know, right? I have to pack and do so much stuff. Anyways, have to go. Love you. Skype tonight?" she asked me, and I agreed.

"Wait, Di, how are you going to get there?" I asked, but deep down, I knew the answer. I knew what she would say.

"By plane." She hesitated, and I knew very well why. My breath caught. My hands started to shake, and my heart started to race. "Astrid, don't be paranoid. I'll be fine."

"You don't know that. You know it's true. She didn't either," I whispered, trying to breathe deeply. I hurried to my room so I could talk to my best friend in private.

"Astrid, please. It's Italy." Diana tried to convince me.

"Just like it was Hawaii to her. You mean the world to me, and I can't lose you too. You have to understand why I'm worried. I'll always be worried." I sat by the bed and looked at my hands.

"I know you're jealous, but why can't you just be happy for me?" She accused. "You went to California, and we heard what a great summer you had. I want to have a great Christmas!"

"I left because I couldn't be here any longer," I said back. "Do you really think it was easy for me to live in this house where she spent so many nights? Her belongings were everywhere. Her pictures were everywhere I looked. It was suffocating me!"

"Yeah, well, now you're suffocating me! 'Look at me! I'm Astrid Bailey, the perfect girl, the girl who guys like Kai pay attention to, the girl who never gets into trouble.'"

"You think my life is perfect? 'Oh no, I'm Diana Kingsey. I'm more popular than you. I'm better than you. One day, I'll become famous, and you'll mean nothing to me. Every guy wants to sleep with me because I always look flawless, and I say yes to them too just because I'm that easy.'" I snapped back at her.

"'Yeah, well, I'm Astrid Bailey, and I also go by the name Ella. I'm the girl who always felt sorry for herself because her best friend died.'"

"You know what? 'I'm Diana Kingsey, and I can't shut up!'" I yelled.

Then I sat there. I sat there in silence, not being able to comprehend what I just did. When it dawned on me that Diana and I had our first real fight ever since we started hanging out again, I cried. I never talked about what happened with her, and she didn't want to either, but saying those things to me made me really mad.

There was a knock on my door, but I ignored it. I ignored the footsteps toward me, and I ignored Addie's worried look. I was mad at Diana. I was mad at myself. Addie sat down on the floor next to my bed and wrapped her arms around me.

"What happened?" she asked in a motherly voice.

"I don't want to talk about it," I replied in a whisper.

"From what I heard, that was the worst fight you two ever had."

I didn't respond. I couldn't. But I decided to let Addie in on the news.

"She's going to Italy," I told her.

"Really? Wow!" Addie said before giving me a confused look. "Is that why you two fought?"

"She's going by plane," I replied.

"Oh." Her mouth formed an 'o' shape.

"I understand how you feel. It can't be easy for you. Diana changed ever since Vanessa died. She wants to do bold stuff. She realized that life is short, and she didn't want to miss out on things. What I'm saying is you two have two completely different points of view, and I'm not saying one is more important or better than the other. But, Astrid, you need to stop living in fear. You're limiting yourself and what you can do. You're not this closed off person. You're one of the brightest, smartest, and nicest people I know. You never used to be like this," she told me as I remained quiet. "You two will work it out," she said in the end and tried to soothe me. This was probably the worst breakdown I had in months.

"Thanks, Addie, but I really want to be alone," I told her, pushing her away.

I wanted to take a bath, lock myself in the bathroom, and read. I wanted to leave this place like I did with California.

"Astrid, I don't think you should be alone right now."

"Please, Addie. Just go. I want to be alone now." I begged her. I was just so emotionally tired. I didn't even listen to myself. All I wanted to do was be alone. I didn't want anybody to see me like this.

"Call me when you calm down, okay? Or I'll call you. I want to make sure you're okay." She stood up.

"Thanks. You're a good friend."

She smiled and left. My brother and his best friends hurried away from the door, desperate not to be seen, but I could hear them all this time.

I closed the door and locked it. The only book that could soothe me in a time like this was *Clockwork Angel*. I didn't know why, but it was one of my go-to books to make me feel better.

Connor came to check up on me a while later. He knocked on the door, but I didn't open up. I was meant to be studying today but didn't feel like it. We would have a test on Tuesday after the winter break, and I would make up for lost time tomorrow. I didn't want to see anybody.

"How are you?" Connor asked through the door. I ignored him. "Astrid, please." He begged me.

I ignored him some more. "I know you're in there, Astrid. I can hear you turning the pages." His comment would usually make me feel a little better, but I was so exhausted and numb, it didn't even bring a smile to my face.

In a way, I missed California. I missed Jessie, Amanda, Ashton, and Daniel. I missed their company a lot.

I heard Mom and Dad shutting both doors of their car. They were home. Connor probably heard that too because he finally decided to leave me alone and go greet them. I wasn't going, though.

Mom called me to dinner. I rejected. Dad came knocking. I pretended to be asleep. Connor tried calling my cell. He got to my voicemail.

The only thing I welcomed right now was the sweet numb feeling of falling asleep.

Chapter 22

I woke up in the afternoon. Connor wasn't at home, and neither were my parents, by the time I came downstairs. There was a Post-it note on the fridge that said I should grab something to eat.

I ignored it. I wasn't hungry. Getting into a fight with Diana—it hurt me. Diana and I never fought. We never said anything bad about each other. What was worse, I regretted everything, but I was also too proud to be the first to apologize. That was always my worst trait. I was too proud, even when it came to Connor.

There was a knock on the front door, and I was the only one home, so it was my responsibility to answer it. I ignored the fact that I looked absolutely worse than usual.

I opened the door and found Matt standing there with food.

"Hey," he said and welcomed himself in.

"Connor's not here," I said as he sat down on the living room couch and put his feet on the coffee table.

"I'm not here to see him," he told me.

"Why are you here then? My parents aren't home," I replied. He seemed to take the hint and took his feet off the coffee table.

"To see you."

"Why?" I raised an eyebrow. What could he ever want with me?

"Connor mentioned you were in a bad state when he left this morning, so he asked me to keep an eye on you."

"Why you?"

"Because I'm the nicest," Matt replied, and I snorted.

"Nathaniel is the nicest. Beck is the funniest. You're just a jerk," I stated.

"Now, now. That's not how you talk to your feeder." Matt *tsk*-ed at me.

"Feeder? What am I, a vampire and you're my blood provider?" I asked sarcastically.

"See, only books would give you that kind of knowledge." He pointed at me.

"So loving to read is suddenly a good thing? Because for as long as I knew, you insulted me for it."

"Why don't you just stop complaining and come eat?" Matt suggested, clearly bored with the conversation.

"No thanks," I said.

"Did you even eat today?" he asked.

"I'm not hungry," I said to him.

"Astrid, Connor put me in charge to take care of you, and I mean to complete my task." He insisted.

"What am I, a dog?" I asked sarcastically again. "I'm not his responsibility, and I can take care of myself. Thank you very much," I said.

"No, you can't. We're all still young, haven't even finished high school. We're basically still kids, and every once in a while, we need somebody to talk to. Especially you since you've been through so much already." Matt scolded me. "Besides, Connor has *us*. He talks to us all the time about it. You don't. You can barely mention her name, and once you do, you start shutting everybody out again. We've seen it happen yesterday, and it will keep on happening if we don't do something about it."

"Did it ever cross your mind I just wanted to be alone?" I responded.

"What kind of person wants to be alone when they feel the weakest?" Matt asked. A proud one, I would've responded. "And after what Kai did…" He didn't continue.

"Why do you think I care about what he did?" I asked.

"Because I've seen the look on your face," Matt said.

"If it was a look of surprise, then you're right. But it was just that, surprise."

"Are you sure?"

"About what?" I pretended to be confused.

"That he didn't hurt you. Are you sure that you didn't feel hurt by his actions?" Matt asked.

"The only person who should be hurt is you. Cindy cheated on you, didn't she? Shouldn't *you* feel mad?" I asked him.

"Cindy is easy. That's why I'm dating her."

"Right," I said. "But that still doesn't make it okay."

"Are you sure you're not upset because you like Kai?" Matt asked me. I was somewhat in denial. I knew I liked him, but I wasn't ready to admit it.

"I don't like him," I replied.

"Good then," Matt said and came closer to me. He was so close that our noses touched. He wrapped an arm around my waist and pulled me under him on the couch. Then he kissed me.

Chapter 23

I returned the kiss, not fully realizing what was happening. The first chance I was able to clear my head, I gently pushed him away.

"Matt, I can't," I said. I wiped my lips with the back of my hand. Matt's chest was still against mine, tracing his finger against my cheek. It was a gentle move.

"Why not?" he had asked me. There was some emotion in his eyes that I couldn't define. His features became tense, and he wouldn't move away. He looked at me, and I knew that if I remained here, it wouldn't mean anything good.

"Because you've treated me like shit my whole life and now you suddenly decide you...what? Like me? Interested? I'm not even sure what's going on here."

"I've liked you for some time, Astrid. You were just too blind to see it."

"Oh, I'm sorry. I didn't know that insulting me was a way of showing how much you like me," I said sarcastically. "Besides, you're my brother's best friend."

"Is that it?" he asked me. "Is that the only reason why?"

"It's also because I don't have those kinds of feelings toward you," I said. I used to, but did that mean I still did?

"Okay then," Matt said and stepped back. "I think I better go." He rushed out before I could say anything. I didn't try to go after him because I knew the whole thing was a mess. I sat down on the floor and rubbed my temples, took deep breaths and tried to calm down for the next five minutes.

I couldn't do anything. I couldn't think. I couldn't sleep. I couldn't eat. Hell, I couldn't even read thanks to the book hangover.

I couldn't stop thinking about Kai.

I thought back when he lied for me just to get Connor off my back, or in the bookstore when he suggested books to read, or when he took me for a ride away from Connor and his friends. Kai was always there when I needed someone. I started to trust him unwillingly.

His brown eyes always fascinated me—or his smile that made him look like a small child, the times he was playful, and the times he kept making sexual remarks.

I dragged my butt to my room and threw myself on my bed. My life was officially a mess, and I couldn't wait for Connor to come home.

"You okay?" I heard a voice ask. I jumped from my bed when I heard him. Kai was standing there, and I hadn't even heard him come through the window.

"What the hell? What are you doing in my bedroom?" I screamed at him.

"You wouldn't answer my calls and reply to my texts. What was I supposed to do?" Kai leaned against the wall.

"Maybe not act like a stalker and creep soundlessly into my bedroom like some vampire," I replied.

"Would you want me to sparkle?" He smirked.

"Like I would want you in any way," I retorted and hopelessly continued our bickering.

"Darling, we both know this is a lie. You're unbelievably attracted to me." He glanced around my room and ran the tips of his fingers across the surface of my desk. He tried to step closer to me, but I moved across the room.

"Are you done making false assumptions?" I smiled sweetly at him. "Because I have much better things to do."

Kai looked at me. I wasn't sure what I was supposed to do. A part of me wanted him here, wanted his arms around me. I wanted him to say everything would be okay.

But before I could do anything stupid, a memory flashed before my eyes: him and Cindy making out, Kai without his shirt on, her skirt pushed halfway up, and her tugging at his pants. He was panting, and she was biting his lip before he pushed her away.

Immediately, I wanted to call Connor and ask him to come home, but I was too upset. Besides, Connor wouldn't give a crap.

But he did send Matt. That was a clear sign he cared, the voice in my head objected.

Kai's smirk disappeared, and he sighed. "I think we need to talk," he said.

"No, we don't. You're the last person I want to talk to right now, so please, just leave me alone." I pointed at the window.

"I thought you didn't care about me," he spoke, clearly trying to prove his point.

"I don't care about you," I said to him.

"It doesn't seem like it. You've ignored both my texts and my calls. You've been avoiding me ever since that party. It doesn't sound like you don't care."

"I had other things to take care of, okay? I'm sorry if you're not the first person that comes to mind."

"Are you sure you're just not jealous?"

"No! That's not what this is about. Not everything is about you, Kai. Just like not everything is about me. I've had things to take care of. If you don't believe me, ask my brother." I snapped.

"Look, I promise I won't do it again, so please just take a deep breath. Otherwise, I won't be able to stop myself because you look adorable when you're jealous."

"Can you just go? I'm not in the mood to do this. Not today."

"Astrid—" he tried to say, but I sent a serious look in his direction.

"As you wish," he said and climbed out of my window.

Chapter 24

Dear Diary,

After Kai had left, I called Nathaniel. Whenever I had a crisis I couldn't solve, he would always be there. I just wanted to hang out with him because right now, he was the only real friend I had left.

I would've called Diana, but we weren't on speaking terms anymore. Adelaide probably had better things to do. Connor was away and wouldn't even care enough to spend time with me, not that I would want his company at the moment. We weren't exactly close, but he *was* my brother. I sighed and walked to the kitchen where I made myself some tea and called Nathaniel.

Picking up the house phone, I called him. He didn't answer. I waited for ten minutes and decided it wasn't worth calling again. He was probably busy, and who would even want to spend time with me after I kept acting like I was on my period?

I went upstairs and was surprised when I heard the doorbell ring. I cautiously went to answer the door and saw Nathaniel standing there.

"Sorry, I didn't pick up. Want some junk food?" he asked with a hopeful smile. This simple gesture made me smile back. I got more junk food in a day than I ever ate in my whole life.

"Oh, come on in, dork," I said and welcomed him in. I so didn't expect his sudden visit. Nathaniel had always been so thoughtful, and I couldn't help but feel safe with him.

"My battery died, and I couldn't call you afterwards because I was out. On the bright side, I decided to bring you some junk food. I figured it was an emergency." He smiled at me as he set down the food and I ruffled his hair.

"You're amazing," I said and hugged him.

"So, what's wrong?" he asked me.

"Nothing, I just need your company today," I told him.

"Ah, so you fell into the dark waters of depression mixed with loneliness and just thought of me as your magnificent saviour." He exaggerated, but I laughed for the first time, and to be honest, my laugh absolutely scared me. My voice was so hoarse, I didn't recognize it.

"Pretty much, yeah."

Then again, Nathaniel made me smile all the time.

"Well, you thought of the right guy because Nath the Magnificent is here to bring you some cheer." I cracked up again. He was such a dork but definitely one of the nicest guys in the group. Whenever I felt down, Nathaniel would do three things: one, bring me junk food; two, make up rhymes because those always crack me up; three, would make me forget about everything that was happening.

With us, we just...were. We existed while all the problems disappeared. That's why I thought he was amazing. Unlike Matt, he didn't throw himself at me today nor push me to talk about everything I wanted to keep to myself.

"Come on, *Nath the Magnificent.*" I teased him and led him to the living room where we watched a movie. It was pretty late when he came to my house, and it would've been a lot later when he was supposed to leave, so he just crashed in my room.

The next morning, Nathaniel and I were woken up by my phone. I answered it.

"Hello?" I asked.

"Hey, sleepyhead. What are you doing?" It was Delilah's cheery voice. I sat up and noticed Nathaniel watching me. Oh God, I must've looked awful. He looked kind of cute with his messy hair, though.

"Sleeping. Why?" I asked her.

"Are you up for some coffee and shopping?" she asked me.

"No," I groaned. I wasn't exactly fond of going out with Delilah. She would usually want to talk about boys and how to lure them in. She would know since she was the bad girl. She wanted to shop before occupying me for the whole day, and then she would usually end it off with a movie in the cinema.

"Come on, Astrid. I heard about what happened from Adelaide, and she knew you needed someone that wasn't exactly in your social group to cheer you up. So you're going to come with me, but before you do, look outside your window." She insisted. "Oh, and no, I'm not waiting outside. Just look."

I did as she told me, and when I walked to the window in my pyjamas, I realized what she was talking about. "It's snowing," I whispered. "Oh my God, it's actually snowing!" I laughed and yelled so loudly, even Nathaniel came to check it out. It was amazing. The snow was everywhere, and the fact it wasn't even that cold made me happy.

But what was so amazing about this was the fact that I only saw snow three times in my life.

"I know! Isn't it incredible?" Delilah asked.

"Yes! I could finally read by the fireplace, and make some cocoa, and experience the perfect reading environment!" I smiled at myself. These were the best reading conditions I could wish for. I loved reading while it was raining outside, but we all knew snow beats it.

"Oh my God, you're such a bibliophile. It's adorable!" Delilah pretended to be irritated and annoyed. "So, are you in?" she asked me then.

"Um, when?" I forced myself not to glance at Nathaniel. Otherwise, he would know something was up.

"In three hours?" she asked.

"Okay. But what time is it, anyway?"

"Seven AM," she said. I groaned.

"You woke me up at seven AM? Seriously?" I asked her. She simply laughed and promised to see me later. I said bye and turned to Nathaniel.

I threw myself on the bed next to him. He smiled at me and rolled over so he was also lying on his stomach.

"I have crazy friends, you know that?"

He laughed under his breath. "Don't we all?" he said.

"True, but I bet your friends don't wake you up in ridiculously early hours."

"Are you kidding? Beck keeps calling me at three AM just to talk about his woman crisis." He laughed.

"What do you mean?" I asked, and he immediately sobered up.

"Nothing," he said.

"Oh, come on, Nath. You know you can't keep anything from me." I batted my eyelashes, and he sighed.

"You're evil, you know that?"

"Yeah, but you love me."

"Sometimes too much," he said, and I punched his arm playfully.

"Spill," I ordered.

"Well, Beck called me a couple nights ago and complained how girls only went for the assholes while the guys who truly cared about them were left ignored," he said. I immediately knew he was talking about me because Nathaniel wouldn't even meet my eyes.

"Maybe the girls don't realize who the assholes are?" I tried to reason. "Or maybe they don't know the nice guys liked them. I guess it truly depends on the situation," I said.

"Yeah, I guess, but it still sucks to see a girl get hurt by someone who didn't deserve her heart in the first place." Nathaniel looked at me. I gave him a sad smile.

"Sometimes all people are stupid, but I know something. Things may be hard, but you just have to wait because they always turn out all right," I told him and sat up. "Now, come on. It's snowing outside, and since we woke up early, we might as well eat breakfast and enjoy the scenery." I dragged him up, and once I made sure he was out of bed, I went to the kitchen.

"So, what are we having?" he asked when I looked in the fridge.

"I don't know." I pretended to be clueless. "Any suggestions?" I raised an eyebrow.

"Can we make pancakes?" he asked. "I never made them before."

I smiled at his child-like enthusiasm and took out eggs and all the other ingredients. "Well then, today is your lucky day," I tried to say in a British accent and thought I did well until Nathan busted out laughing. "What?" I asked, feeling a little offended.

"You suck at the British accent," he managed to tell me.

"I do not!" I put the ingredients on the counter, and he still wouldn't stop laughing. "You know what? Feel free to make pancakes by yourself." I stomped off. That seemed to force him to stop laughing. He ran after me and apologized. When I saw the amusement in his eyes, I caved in. It was impossible to say no to Nathaniel. We made pancakes and had fun. I even threw some flour at him, just like in the movies, and couldn't stop laughing at his face.

We finished eating at eight-thirty AM. Nathaniel mentioned yesterday that he had to be home by nine because the guys were going to hang out. So I said goodbye to him and cleaned the house a little—yes, even Connor's room.

Then I got ready to meet Delilah. I was ten minutes early when I arrived at McDonald's. It wasn't busy. In fact, I believed most people were either at home sleeping, outside playing in the snow, or shopping. Nobody was thinking about breakfast at McDonald's. Although I've already had breakfast, I still ordered a double cheeseburger.

Today was one of those days I was craving for food.

Delilah and I talked about the last few days, and I told her about everything that happened with Matt, Kai, Nathaniel, and Diana. She waited for me to finish before she spoke.

"You know what you need?" she asked. "I think since New Year's coming closer and closer, you might as well get a makeover to relax."

Diana and Delilah loved makeovers, and while they relaxed them, I always felt somewhat uneasy with them. Something about changing your comfortable way of living set alarms in my mind. I really disliked changes, and that was what made me even more surprised when I said yes.

"Okay," I told her. We were in the mall, and there were shops everywhere.

"You serious?" She raised an eyebrow.

"Oh, what the hell, let's do it."

Chapter 25

This was my first time getting a makeover, and if you thought makeovers were fun, you were wrong.

For hours, I had to walk around shops to look at some clothes, and when I was finally able to sit down for a minute, Delilah found some other shops she wanted to take me to. My mom and dad gave me some money so I could buy as many things as I wanted. It was their way of saying happy way-too-early birthday, considering my birthday was in August.

Delilah and I bought many clothes. They were a lot classier than my usual sweats or faded jeans. She only picked out clothes that made me stand out, but knowing my anxiety problems, she didn't go over the top.

Feeling like a girly girl, I let Delilah drag me to the spa after we were finished. She made appointments, and this part, she said, was on her. We had waxing done, our eyebrows fixed, and massages done. They even offered hair treatments, and everything you would usually take care of in a hair salon.

My dark brown hair got cut a bit and received an ombre because Delilah thought it would be a nice change, something that would make my features stand out a bit more.

Sometimes, I wished I was more like Delilah. She didn't seem to care about what others thought, and she was fearless. Spending this day with her made me feel less alone. I felt comforted with her company, yet I was surprised Delilah wanted to spend time with me outside of school.

When I was allowed to look in the mirror, I found myself speechless. My hair was a little shorter than it was before. It was also lighter and weighed less. I fell in love with it immediately. I ran my fingers through my hair and felt just how soft it was.

"She looks like she just found out what love at first sight means," Gregory, the hair stylist, said to Delilah. She smiled at him.

Then we paid, said goodbye, and left for Delilah's house. It would be the first time I actually visited it when there was no party. I texted Connor I was not going to be home tonight even though I knew he wouldn't be either.

Where are you going to be then? he texted me back two minutes later.

@ Delilah's, I texted back.

K was his reply.

"Hey, you know what you should do?" she asked when she drove the car. It was still snowing, and I was happy that it was, but the cold wasn't taking any pity on me. I was putting my new coat on as I answered Delilah's question with my own.

"No, what?"

She took a right turn and drove into her driveway. We walked inside her house, carrying my bags, when she finally decided to answer as we sat down on her bed.

"You should take a selfie and post it on Facebook and Instagram," she said.

"No, thanks. You know how much I hate taking pictures," I told her, and it was true.

"You have to! Please? For me? How else are your friends going to see your new look?" She tried to convince me when I really wanted to say, *What friends?*

In the end, it took twenty minutes of begging and one pizza to make me change my mind. I was starving since we spent all our time outside taking care of our looks instead of taking care of our hunger.

Delilah, of course, wouldn't let me eat before I took the damn picture, so I was kind of in a hurry. Starvation was a real deal with me. In the end, I took my phone, found the perfect filter, posed, and snapped a picture just so she would leave me alone. When she saw the picture, she squealed then took my phone from me.

"Hey!" I objected but saw her slide a box of pizza to me. "Oooh, pizza." And just like that, I completely forgot about my phone as I dove in.

After a few seconds, Delilah put my phone down and sighed. "There. All done," Delilah told me, and then started texting someone from her own phone.

"What are you doing?" I said, stuffing myself with a third slice.

"I posted your photo with the caption: *When Delilah Washington takes over, you get a makeover.*"

"That's not even funny. Why would you write that caption? I'm going to look like an idiot," I said. "What are you doing *now?*"

"Now, I've liked your photo, and I've texted every single person in school to check out how hot you look," she said.

"Delilah!" I snapped. This was *not* a way for me to stay invisible.

"What?" she asked innocently.

"Stop, okay? I know what you're doing, and it's not going to work," I said. She was trying to show people who insulted me every day at school. "Besides, Connor's going to go ballistic."

"Actually, no," she said.

"What?"

"He commented on your picture, and it has fifty-seven likes already." I abandoned my pizza as she turned on her laptop and let me log onto my Facebook account.

"Unbelievable," I whispered as I scrolled through all the notifications.

"I know, right?" she said. I opened my picture and read the comments.

Somebody commented they had *'never realized I looked beautiful'* which made me just a bit uncomfortable.

Kai's friend Mason Zachary actually tagged Connor as he wrote, *'Now I know why you chase guys away from your sister ;)'*

My brother only replied with *'Stay away from her.'*

Simple but firm. That's how my brother was. I rolled my eyes at his comment. I noticed Matt liked the picture but didn't comment on it. Nathaniel, on the other hand, did.

I didn't reply to any of them, and the picture kept getting more and more likes. I got more and more friend requests, *but* for some reason, I felt like something had changed.

And for the first time in years, I didn't feel like a social outcast.

Chapter 26

Dear Diary,

I came home the next day, totally not expecting what was about to happen. But it did, and before I gave anything away, here's the full story.

The first thing I did when I got home was take all the bags to my room. Then, I changed my clothes and put on some makeup because I felt like it.

With music playing through my earphones, I walked down the kitchen and opened the fridge. I stood there for about ten seconds and got absolutely frightened when I closed it. Connor and his friends were standing there, all watching me like some creeps, making me jump. They were a mess.

"Guys! You scared the living shiz out of me." I scolded them, but they all seemed to be speechless by my new look. Matt was staring with his mouth halfway open. Nathaniel smiled, and Beck just started twirling my hair around his finger like a little child. Connor was the first one to speak, though.

"You look great," he told me. Connor rarely gave me compliments, but when he did, they weren't really that special. Sorry to burst his bubble, but it was true.

"Ignore him. You look more than great." Nathaniel was still smiling. There was something weird going on between the guys, and I couldn't quite decide what it was.

"The new hair colour really brings out your eyes," Matt told me like it pained him.

Connor coughed a few times before saying anything else. "I must say, I'm happy you're home."

"We're starving," Connor continued, and I raised my eyebrow.

"Do I look like your personal chef?"

"No, you look like a model, and I thought we covered this last night and today," he replied, talking about the picture. "But no pizza delivery guy's going to bring us pizzas in this storm, so you're our only option."

It was true. There was a huge blizzard outside.

"Why? Can't you cook?" I asked as I took a sip of the water I just poured in my glass.

"You know the time I almost burned the house down?" he whispered as if it were embarrassing.

"Good point," I replied before turning to the rest of them. "Sit down, guys, and tell me, what do you suggest I make?" I clapped my hands and quickly glanced over to Connor.

"I want eggs!" my brother said. "You know, the ones you make with bacon, toast, and cheese. Those are my favourite!"

Yeah, that was the only thing that got him excited when it came to me. He convinced the guys to try my "specialty," as he would call it, and in the end, I had to make that for all of them. I put on my music and sang out loud.

Connor commented on it later. "You really should've gone to New York when you had the chance. You know Mom would've let you."

"Trying to get rid of me?" I mock-gasped.

"You know that's not what I mean. You're a great singer. You should've gone to a proper music school."

"Yeah…no." I chuckled. "I'm not nearly half as good as them, you know that. Besides, I would probably get myself kidnapped in a city as big as New York. You know I always have the worst of luck." I smiled to myself as I brought them their breakfast. Then I started making coffee.

"Anyone wants some coffee?" I asked.

"Since when do you drink coffee?" Beck looked at me weirdly.

"Since this summer," I replied before I took my cup of coffee with me as I sat down. "I didn't know you guys were going to be here this early," I spoke as they ate. Connor managed to swallow and answer.

"When you texted us, we decided to crash here instead of Matt's place. Is it okay with you if they sleep over today too?" Connor raised an eyebrow.

"Since when do you ask me for my opinion?"

"Since you pointed out so subtly what a horrible brother I've been."

"Well, it's the truth," I replied. "But do whatever you want because I'll stay out of your way."

I went on my phone a bit and accidentally stumbled upon an old picture.

"Astrid?"

"Huh?" I looked up from my cup of coffee.

"You keep smiling to yourself. It's creepy." Connor commented, which I chose to ignore.

I decided to give the guys some space later, so I excused myself and went to my room. When I stepped inside, I almost didn't see Kai standing in the middle of it. My heart did a backflip. It skipped a beat, and the butterflies came alive.

But I had to ignore that feeling because he was here. I wanted to act at least a little sane.

"Dude, you really need to stop sneaking into my ro—" I started to say, but he cut me off with a kiss.

Chapter 27

I had no idea what went through my mind when Kai kissed me. All I knew was that I started to kiss him back. He was a wonderful kisser. His lips were soft but tender, and the way he kissed me was something I couldn't resist. Maybe that was why I kissed him back; I don't know.

Kai pulled back from me, and looking into his eyes, I immediately knew the reason. I had missed him a lot.

He leaned his forehead on mine and closed his eyes.

"Please, don't be mad at me. I can't stand it," he whispered, cupping my cheeks. My hands met his, and I had to pull them away from me. When he realized what was happening, his hands dropped to the side.

"Kai." My voice came out as a weak squeal. "I'm not mad, but please don't do this," I told him. I knew I couldn't resist him. He was the kind of guy who was irresistible.

"Astrid, you have no idea how painful it is for me to stay away. I can't be without you. I need you." He confessed.

"You need me?" I whispered.

Kai nodded. "I know you told me over and over again that you don't care, but I really like you. And I want to be with you. I want to be the gentleman you deserve."

I was speechless because all of this seemed to be surreal. He looked tired with dark circles under his eyes, and I was suddenly worried.

"I don't know what to say."

I never had a boyfriend. I didn't know what I would do with a boyfriend, anyway. I would probably be like: *Should I feed it? Does it drink? What do I do if it's upset? Should I just pat its head and say, "There, there?"*

Snapping me out of my thoughts, Kai spoke, "I want to be more than friends."

There was a spark of hope in his eyes as I walked over to my bed and sat down. My breathing became wilder as he sat down beside me. He took my hands in his, and the gesture forced me to look at him.

"When did you last sleep?" I asked, taking in the way he looked.

"I don't remember. I just missed you a lot."

Knowing the guys were downstairs, I got up and locked the door. When I turned around, I also saw his room was empty, but there was only a light turned on. "Go to your room," I ordered him.

"What?" Surprise was written all over his face.

"Just go turn off the lights and then come back here."

A few moments later, he climbed through the window, stepped on the thick tree branch, and got into his room. When he came back, I was already under the covers. Yesterday's events had exhausted me.

"Come here and lie down next to me."

That made his eyebrows rise. "Not for that reason, you idiot." I laughed.

He took off his shoes and slid under the covers next to me. I turned to my side so I could look at him.

"Tomorrow's New Year, and you should really get some rest," I told him. He rested my head on his shoulder, so I was in his embrace as he started playing with my hair. Eventually, those little movements stopped as his breathing steadied.

I knew he was asleep then. It didn't take him long, only ten to fifteen minutes. I snuggled up to him, and soon, I was fast asleep as well.

When I woke up, Kai was still sleeping. My phone had started to ring, and knowing it was across the room, I had to stand up to take it.

I pulled away from Kai, thinking he was still asleep when his hand wrapped around my arm.

"Don't go," he spoke in a sleepy voice.

"I'll be right back." I slid out of bed and walked barefoot across the room. Adelaide was calling me.

"Addie?" I asked, surprised.

"Astrid, you need to see this," she said. "Turn on your computer."

I did as I was told but still complained. "What's so important that made you call me?" I asked.

"Shut up and look at your notifications!" It was clear Adelaide was happy. "Congrats," she said and then hung up without an explanation. As soon as my computer let me log on to Facebook, I clicked on my notifications.

My picture was shared by a Facebook page called Instagram Celebrities with the caption written: *"Astrid Bailey is our newest obsession."*

As I went on my Instagram, I was shocked to see I received over six thousand followers. Kai showed up by my side just as I gasped. He wrapped his arms around my waist as he looked at my phone. This gesture made my heart melt, but I couldn't comprehend what was happening.

I got noticed by more people than I wanted, and it was all Delilah's idea. I only had three pictures up on my Instagram, but that seemed to be enough for me to attract attention.

"Is that you?" Kai asked, pointing at the post Instagram Celebrities had shared.

"Yes," I said, half-crying and half-laughing. "They shared my picture, and now I got thousands of followers overnight."

Kai smiled softly, and my breath caught as he kissed my cheek. My back was against his chest, and I felt butterflies in my stomach. I could feel electricity where we touched.

"I told you that you're beautiful, and you're the only person who doesn't see it yet."

"You think too highly of me."

"The moment you stop feeling insecure is the moment I'll be the happiest guy alive," Kai told me honestly before taking my hand and dragging me back to bed.

Chapter 28

Kai and I slept through the whole day and the next morning when I woke up before him. My door was still locked, and I wanted to keep it that way because no way in hell would I let my brother or his friends come in and see Kai sleeping over.

I picked out an outfit from my closet and headed towards the bathroom. I took a quick shower before walking out of the bathroom. As I was combing through my hair, I heard Kai wake up and yawn loudly.

"Good morning," I greeted him with a smile.

"Morning," he replied, a few signs of sleep evident on his face. He looked so much like a small child. I liked his face when he wasn't all arrogant and smirking all the time. It made him pretty good-looking; I would admit that.

Before he even noticed I was staring, I turned away and continued to brush my hair. "Don't tell me you got ready just to impress me."

And there it was. Really, with Kai, you couldn't expect his arrogance and cockiness to stay away too long.

"As if you're worth impressing," I told him in a joking manner. Kai smirked.

"If you're not amazed by my face, there's some other guy I know who might impress you." He winked, and because of my dirty mind, I immediately caught on his train of thought.

"Sure, whatever you say." I laughed it off because, honestly, I had no idea what to say to that.

I was sitting at the desk by the window, looking at a small mirror, and couldn't decide whether to put my hair up or down because my attention was on Kai.

"It suits you better if you leave your hair down," he told me then walked over. "Forgot to compliment your new look, by the way," he whispered in my ear as his hands played with my hair.

"That wasn't a compliment either," I replied with a blank face.

"Okay, if you must. You look more than gorgeous. Happy?" There was an amused look in his deep brown eyes that I loved dearly.

I smiled proudly, put my chin up, and said jokingly, "I know." Kai chuckled.

"Who's the big-headed jerk now?" he asked me.

"Hey! I didn't call you a jerk," I said, reminding him about the dinner we had together when his family was invited to our house.

"No, but you did say my head was big," Kai stated.

Okay, I might've said that. So much about that was true, and I couldn't help but think to myself how much I still didn't know about Kai. I basically knew as much as I knew back then.

"Certainly not as big as your ego," I replied again, and he laughed—that warm, hearty laugh that sent goosebumps down my arms.

"It's true, though," I said.

"Maybe, but you love me," he replied.

"Oh, I wouldn't go that far, Kai." I scoffed.

"Not yet," he said as he picked up one of his T-shirts he changed into yesterday then headed through the window.

Once he was in his room, he called my name.

"Astrid?" He was leaning against the window frame.

I turned to him and did the same thing.

"What?" I asked innocently.

"But you will."

Not yet…But you will.

Chapter 29

Dear Diary,

It was six hours until New Years. Connor invited his friends over—the whole football team—and I invited mine. In the end, there was quite a crowd gathered in our living room, and Kai was one of the people invited.

Mom and Dad came home to make food for us, but after that, they went to their friend's house just like they did every year. I know that by the amount of time we saw each other, people would think they would want to spend every second near us, but it wasn't like that. They wanted Connor and me to become independent, and we understood that from a very young age. Through those years, Connor just grew apart with them while I still hugged my mom and kissed my dad's cheek. I was a good girl who loved her parents dearly.

After the parentals had left, the guys transformed the dining room table into a beer pong table. It was such a typical guy thing to do though this wouldn't be a party. It was just guys hanging out.

I ignored Kai, and he ignored me, but it was Matt who kept stealing glances at me when he thought I didn't notice. When the other guys from the football team saw me, their mouths dropped, and I wanted to hide.

I shyly said hi to the visitors as I walked into the kitchen and opened the fridge. However, I still heard them whisper.

"Whoa, your sister is so hot!" one of them said.

"I would totally bang her," the other one added. I ignored them and looked for more alcohol because I would need it if I was going to get through this night. What? With my house filled with people? The guys had beer, but I had something else in mind.

"Connor?" I turned to him. He was watching me intently. "Do we have any vodka left?"

"Why?" He eyed me suspiciously.

"Oh, come on, dear brother. You can't really expect a girl to give away all her secrets now, can you?" I leaned forward on the counter and placed my chin atop my knuckles, in a pose that showed slight interest.

"Oh, please, Astrid. Like you have any secrets." He chuckled.

"Um, to remind you that talk we had a while ago..." I reminded him about the sex talk. There was a bit of silence between my insinuation and his response.

"You're unbelievable," he said and sighed.

"I think there's no need to state the obvious." I smiled sweetly at Connor as the guys looked at what was happening. Yes, I always became cocky when I needed something from Connor, but that was usually the way we interacted.

"Come on." Connor led me to the liquor cabinet where we kept our drinks, and he handed over the vodka.

"Thanks. Do you have anything to mix it with?" I asked him. Connor gave me a weird look but did as I asked. In the end, all

I had to do was wait for the girls, then we were going to be in my room.

"You're not going to celebrate with us?" Beck sounded almost disappointed.

"Nope," I said, popping the 'p.' "It's tradition."

"Whose idea was that stupid tradition, anyway?" Matt objected.

"That would be yours," Connor pointed at Matt.

"Don't worry, guys," I said. "I'm much happier being upstairs than hanging out with a bunch of people I don't even like," I replied honestly before I disappeared into my room. All those people in my house always gave me a hard time in school, so I was not going to sweeten my feelings for them.

Besides, the guys played their beer pong or gossiped over which girl's the hottest and ugliest. I despised their talks because not only were they hurtful but also disrespectful.

Adelaide and Delilah finally arrived. Diana was with them. When I headed down the stairs to answer the door, Connor already beat me to it.

"Hey!" Addie rushed to hug me, and I hugged her back.

"Oh, I missed you so much," I said to them as I hugged Delilah and Adelaide. Things got a little awkward when it came to Diana.

"Look—" I started.

"No, Astrid, please. I need to say this first," Diana said. "Everything I said to you was in anger. I'm sorry. I didn't mean any of it, and you didn't deserve to hear that. I was selfish and unbelievably cruel. You were just worried about me, and I'm sorry for yelling at you like that. I know it was awful of me, and if you could ever forgive me, I would be truly grateful."

"Oh, come here." I hugged her. "I'm sorry too. I didn't mean to say all those things or yell at you. I realize that I was paranoid, but I regretted hanging up on you. I still hope Italy was amazing." Diana gave me a slight kiss on the cheek when we departed from each other's hold.

"It was," she said, and I smiled. "Friends?" Diana asked and put up her pinkie. I did the pinkie swear with her and replied, "Friends."

"Finally," Delilah and Addie said at the same time. Right before we wanted to head up the stairs, Connor stopped us.

"Before you go, Mom baked something that she wants us to share," he said, gesturing us to the kitchen. Ah, he was talking about Mom's masterpiece. They were her famous chocolate chip muffins. Everyone adored them. Mom was the queen of baking.

Adelaide and Diana rushed to the kitchen, not expecting to see a group of guys from school standing there. Every year, I used to hide in my room from them. Usually, Connor would order me to stay there, but eventually, when I realized what kind of assholes my brother's friends were, I chose to stay behind closed doors and inside the safety of my room.

My friends and I were, however, spending our first New Years together. The guys may have known them from school, but not everyone.

I waited as the girls took their muffins and made conversation with me.

"Did you hear from that Jessie girl lately?" Delilah asked me, not sure why she was wondering.

"Yeah, she drunk-texted me last week. Something about her and Daniel kissing."

Delilah knew almost everything about my summer in California. I called her often when I missed my home. Connor was too busy for me, and my parents kept working, while all my friends never picked up. So she heard almost every single story about my stay there.

"Wow," she said, surprised.

"Who's Jessie?" Diana asked.

"One of my closest friends," I replied, which didn't make Diana any happier, but she didn't push me.

"I still don't know who Luke is," Connor chimed in, and I gave him a pointed look.

"And you never will," I said back.

"You're impossible," he replied.

"I learned from the best," I responded. As soon as the girls ate their muffins, we went upstairs where they started interrogating me about my full house.

"I had no idea what you meant when you said every single popular guy from school was at your house," Diana said. "Why didn't you invite us sooner?"

"No, more importantly," Addie corrected, "why aren't you spending time with them?"

"Because I have no interest in doing that."

"Why not?" Diana pushed me.

"Because they're guys. They make inappropriate jokes, rate girls' boobs and ass on a scale of one to ten, and make a list of the most bang-worthy girls. Not to mention how pushy they are when they get drunk. Oh, and one more little detail: they all made my life a living hell. So no, thank you."

"You're such a party-pooper," Diana complained while crossing her arms.

"Nope, I'm just looking out for myself, and I'm trying to be realistic," I said. I had no idea how to act around guys. I would honestly need a dictionary and a crap-load of confidence to survive the New Years with the guys downstairs.

"You could never be realistic. You're too caught up in your own world to know what's going on around you," Adelaide replied.

"True, but I've got experience from the last few years, which is more than I could say for you," I replied.

"Fine," Diana said. "Is there any booze?" I pointed to the vodka, and she smiled.

"Girls," she said. "Let's get this party started."

Chapter 30

Dear Diary,

The next day when I woke up, I regretted my decision to get drunk almost immediately. For starters, I woke up on the dining room table. Lifting my head, I felt searing pain attack my brain. It was like a hangover, but ten times worse than anything I'd ever experienced. How did I end up here? What happened?

Sitting up, I noticed the messed up state my house was in. There were empty bottles of alcohol everywhere. Toilet paper was on the floor. Shoes and clothes were everywhere, and the only thing I could remember was it all started with vodka.

Oh, and somehow, I found peanuts everywhere—even in my bra.

Sliding myself off the dining table, I felt the intense need to puke. My head was throbbing, and I felt dizzy enough as it was. Heading towards the bathroom, I opened the door, and in front of me was Connor sleeping in the bathtub. This thing alone made me wake up, and I didn't have to puke anymore.

Instead, I walked over to Connor and shook his shoulder.

He mumbled something in his sleep and turned around. I did it harder, this time by actually calling his name. "Connor?" His eyes fluttered open, and he looked at me like I was some weird alien creature until his eyes focused on me.

"Astrid?" he asked me in a sleepy yet confused voice. "What the hell happened?" He took in his surroundings as he asked the question we were both asking ourselves.

"I have no idea."

Whoa, my voice was hoarse. I could barely talk, and maybe that was the reason my throat hurt so much. "Come on. We need to find out everything about last night," I said, grabbing Connor's hand and pulling him out of the bathtub.

Connor groaned as I made him follow me out of the bathroom, but he came to a halt when he saw the state our house was in.

"What *the hell* happened?" he now asked in a way more serious tone. I met his eyes and shrugged.

"You go check out your room. I'll go check out mine," I instructed, rubbing my temples. Connor and I split up, and I headed towards my bedroom. I opened the door with difficulty, and when I did, the sight in front of me made me scream.

"What did you do to my room?"

Addie, Diana, Beck, and Nathaniel who were all sharing my bed immediately jumped up and looked around them, startled. I was furious.

My wall was covered in toilet paper. There were sticky notes everywhere, and not to mention that someone spray-painted 'I LOVE OREOS' on my wall.

What. The. Fuck.

"What did you do to my room?" I asked them in an accusing voice.

"Oh" was all that Beck let out. He scratched the back of his head and looked at everything but me.

"Well?" I pushed them to tell me.

"You don't remember?" Diana spoke.

What were they talking about?

"Remember what?" I asked.

Beck smirked. "Check your Facebook," he replied as they gathered their stuff and walked out of my room.

"Hey! Who's going to clean up all this?" I called after them but did not push it because this Facebook thing really got me curious. I uncovered my laptop from everything that was on it and plugged it in for the battery to charge. I was finally able to log into Facebook when my phone rang.

"Hello?" I answered. My head still throbbed, and I made a mental note to take some aspirin.

"Astrid?" I heard the voice on the other end say.

"Matt?" I was surprised to see him calling me. "Are you okay?" He seemed strange.

"No. I know you said you didn't like me, but you didn't have to be such a bitch about it," Matt said and hung up.

What on Earth was going on?

Is this how I was going to spend January 1? Because if the answer was yes, then I might as well quit trying to find answers and take some time to read as a way to isolate myself from all the drama. With no recollection of what happened yesterday, I focused my attention back to my computer in hopes of stirring my memory.

As I scrolled down the notifications—a couple of them tagging me and me thanking them for providing the craziest party ever—one post caught my eye.

It was Kai's. When had I accepted his friend request? Oh, but things were going to get more interesting.

Because Kai added me as his girlfriend on Facebook, and he uploaded a picture of us kissing.

Immediately, I picked up my phone and called him. After hundreds of rings, there was no answer, so I decided to go look for him.

All I could remember were glimpses of last night. I knew Addie forced Diana and me to go down and hang out with the guys, but the next thing I remembered was me lying on the dining table and one of the boys doing shots off me. Was it Kai? Matt?

Oh, no. I think it was Beck. Ahh!

I hurried to the kitchen, and on my way there, I bumped into someone.

"Sorry," I muttered, but the person I bumped into was probably in a worse state than me. As I glanced up, I saw Kai standing there, smirking a little. He was obviously still a little drunk. Actually, we all were, but we were sober enough to feel hung-over.

Still, that didn't stop me from noticing Kai's left eye was bruised. What happened? I had no idea.

"Hey, are you okay?" I asked him and slightly touched his eye. He shrugged off my hand.

"I'm fine." He wanted to head out the door, but I took his hand and stopped him.

"What happened?" I asked.

"You don't remember?" Kai looked at me in surprise.

"I don't remember anything," I said while shaking my head.

"Look it up on Facebook," he said and turned around. This time, I grabbed his hand even more tightly and didn't let him go.

"Why does everybody keep saying that? I already looked on Facebook, and what does that help me when it doesn't make any sense?" I yelled at Kai, clearly frustrated. He was taken aback, but I wanted to know the truth. Finally, he sighed and took me to my room.

He sat down on the bed and motioned me to sit down beside him.

"Yesterday, you drank way too much by the time you came downstairs, and you wanted to party. So, the night began. We did more shots. You were too drunk. Then we danced some more, and it all ended with New Year's," he said, but that still didn't make any sense.

"But what about the pictures? My room? Toilet paper? Peanuts? Your black eye?" I questioned him. "And why was Connor sleeping in the bathtub?"

Kai chuckled. "Nothing ever gets past you, does it?" I gave him an annoyed look, which made him sigh. "Alright. We were trying to wrap Mason in toilet paper to see if he could move. But it didn't work, so he started chasing us around, and we ended up having a toilet paper fight. A bowl of peanuts may have gotten in the way, and you thought peanuts were rice and that Diana and Beck were getting married. You started throwing it at them, and they started running."

Wait, what?

"Why would I think that?" I scowled.

"Because they were making out," Kai explained.

"What!" I gave him a shocked look. "Di and Beck?" It seemed almost impossible.

"Yeah, but they were both drunk, so I wouldn't think anything of it," Kai told me. "What else?"

"My room...Black eye?" I pointed at his eye. Kai's expression suddenly got serious.

"I wrote that," he said, pointing at the wall. Suddenly, a memory came rushing back. Kai saying something...

"Prove it." I could barely say the two words properly. *Was my right hand bigger than my left? Why did we need fingers? Kai looked so sexy when he was drunk.*

"How?" he said, the word slurred. *That made me focus my attention back to what we were talking about. Kai said he loved me. He was probably joking, but I pretended to believe him only to see how far he was going to take this.*

"Spray-paint 'I LOVE OREOS' on my wall." I challenged him.

"Where am I going to get spray paint?" he asked me.

"I don't care. That's your problem," I muttered.

"You said…"

"Yeah," he said. "I was drunk."

There was a small blush spreading through his cheeks, but he tried to hide it by tilting his head away from me.

"You know that children and drunk people are the most honest people in the world, right?" I stated.

"You confessed to me that you like to sleep naked. Is that true then?" He smirked and looked at me.

"I did not! And I do not!" I looked outraged. "Stop lying and trying to divert the topic away from me," I scolded. "What about your black eye?"

Kai tensed up beside me. I was grateful he even decided to fill me in this far.

"We were getting pretty comfortable after I spray-painted that. When Matt asked you what was that writing on the wall, you told him about us, and he decided to punch me. After that, I wanted to leave. I only stayed because you asked me to. I don't know about the rest, though."

"Does it hurt? Your eye, I mean."

"Eh, it's okay." Kai stood up to walk out of my room, but I stopped him one last time.

"Why are we in a relationship on Facebook?" I asked him.

"Because when we were both drunk, I asked you to be my girlfriend to which you agreed."

He walked to me and gave me a kiss before he left.

Chapter 31

Wassup, Diary?

Just thought I'd change things up a bit. Kissing Kai was probably one of the most amazing things I had done. Even though it was all I could think of, I couldn't help but feel a little mad that he asked me to be his girlfriend when I was drunk. Actually, that was a good call because there was no guarantee I would have agreed if I was sober.

See, Kai was infuriating, frustrating, intense, and testosterone-filled. He gave off the vibe of being possessive, and as much as I liked him—I won't lie; he was one of those guys every single girl fell for—I still didn't want to be just some side chick to him.

I decided that a makeover wasn't going to suffice. I needed to get myself a backbone if bad boys were going to be in my life.

The only way I saw that happening was to organize my life again. I dived back into my book blog which had been quite abandoned for months. I had been filming new videos and talked more about books. I also had to repaint my room because I was not going to have an 'I LOVE OREOS' sign on my walls. That also led me to redecorate my entire bedroom, and I had never felt better. A clean living space made me feel more comfortable and happier with myself.

So this was how I spent my last few days, and too soon, it was time to go back to school. My alarm clock rang at five AM, and I managed to get up fully relaxed for a change. I hopped right into the shower and was not in a hurry. I did my morning routine and headed down to eat some breakfast, finally settling down for some cereal.

Connor was nowhere to be found. I guess he wanted to skip school today or he just fell asleep. Either way, I was going to mind my own business like always and leave him alone. Trust me, nobody wanted to face his wrath in the morning. He was like Lucifer's own child, waiting to burn the whole world down.

I put my earphones in and cleaned the dishes. I was so focused on the task at hand, I almost didn't feel the tap on my shoulder. I dried my hands as I turned around.

My mom and dad were home!

"I missed you so much!" I spoke, hugging them both.

"Oh, we missed you too, sweetheart." My mom almost shed a tear.

"We wanted to see you and Connor more, so we took some time off work. I hope that's okay," Dad said in his deep, serious voice.

"Are you kidding? That's amazing!" I said.

"Where is Connor, anyway?" Mom asked. I just shrugged.

"Beats me, but if he's still asleep, I'm not going up there to wake him up. I'm going to be stuck with him in school all day, so I don't really want to face his rage."

Mom gave me a he's-your-brother look. Yes, he may be my brother, but I was still not going to risk it.

"I'll go. I'll talk to him," Dad said, and I gave him a kiss on the cheek.

My mom had me sit down. I had twenty more minutes to kill, so I could talk to her.

"Is everything okay?" I asked her, worried because she looked extra tired. The bags under her eyes didn't help her appearance.

"Life's so exhausting." She didn't answer my question.

"Mom," I said a little too loudly. I hated it when Mom changed the subject. "Tell me," I whispered in the end.

"Grandma Elaine is coming to visit us next week."

That was her mother. Grandma Elaine was the coolest grandma I ever had. She liked to buy me books. We read together, and we both used to annoy Connor and Grandpa so much.

"How come?" I asked.

"Honey," she spoke and then took a deep breath. "Grandpa died," Mom said sadly.

"What?" I didn't know what to say. This couldn't be happening. Not my grandpa. Not him.

"When?" I finally asked softly.

"He died last night. The funeral will be on Friday, and it will be hosted here. Grandma will be living with us from now on, and she'll be your babysitter for the next four weeks."

"Why four weeks?" There were tears in my eyes—tears that I didn't want to fall down my cheek.

"Because your dad and I are going to sell your grandparents' house, and we are going to stay there for a bit."

One tear just dropped. My heart sank. My hands shook. I was really close to my grandparents though it may not have seemed like it.

I was still in shock, so the only thing I could say was okay. I went to my room and sobbed. I was not in the mood to talk to anyone today, and I could already feel it. I grabbed a book to occupy myself and stormed out of the house. I took the bus to school, and while watching the houses and trees go by, I sank into the deep oblivion, feeling the sorrow overtake my body. I couldn't breathe. It was like the whole world was playing a game on me. My whole world was crashing down worse than ever before. All that was left of me was a girl so broken inside, and she just wanted to cry, but she wouldn't. She would keep herself busy. She wouldn't let her walls down, and she would definitely stay strong.

I went through this once. I already knew how to deal with grief.

Chapter 32

Arriving at school, I didn't talk to anybody. When Diana called my name, I didn't respond. When Addie tried to make me notice her, I ignored her. People were giving me weird looks. One of the cheerleaders even came up to me.

"Wow, who died?" she said, and other cheerleaders laughed, but the only thing that it did was bring tears to my eyes. Soon, they realized that someone *had* actually died.

I passed more people through the halls, and they all seemed to whisper things about me.

"So pathetic," someone said.

"Is the nerd actually crying?" One chuckled.

"She's annoying the living shit out of me."

"Do I even have to look at her?" a popular girl asked.

"I wish she'd just go home," the other said in agreement.

I hurried to the bathroom after that and sobbed. For a moment, I thought things would change, that people would notice I was a human being who can get hurt, who *they* kept hurting. I was dumb enough to believe Kai and everything he told me. I actually thought I made some friends, but it was all pretend.

I was utterly and completely alone.

"Astrid?" Delilah's voice echoed through the bathroom. "I know you're here. Are you okay?"

I kept quiet. Slowly, I wiped my tears from my eyes.

"Connor told me what happened. Are you okay?" she asked again.

Since when was she in touch with Connor? They never really got along.

"I'm not leaving until you talk to me," she said, and I believed her. Delilah was determined, stubborn, and one hell of a listener. This wasn't something I could talk about, though.

"I'm fine." My voice came out hoarse, and it was evident I was crying.

"If this is about the cheerleaders, ignore them. You know they're bitches. They're not worth your time." She tried to console me. My hands were shaking, and I shivered so much that I started to tremble. "Come out, Astrid."

"Just go. I need to be alone for a minute, okay? Don't worry about me."

"Suit yourself, but I'm not going to class until you come out," she told me and left. I breathed out a short sigh of relief because soon, another door opened with a creak.

"Did you hear what happened?" a girl said.

"Connor's grandpa died? Poor him." She didn't even sound sorry. "I bet he won't even come to school. Oh, how sad he must be feeling right now."

"Did you see his sister this morning?" another one asked as the first girl laughed.

"Completely pathetic," she said. I barely contained my tears as I started to shake even more. That truly hurt. "She thinks that her victimized look will get her anywhere. I'm so tired of seeing her face every day."

"She doesn't even deserve to have a brother as perfect as him. She's such a loser. I have no idea what Kai sees in her."

"He probably pities her like the rest of the school. You know, the whole 'oh, my best friend died years ago, let me put on my puppy dog eyes and follow around every single guy I find' thing."

"I know, right? Pathetic doesn't even begin to describe what she is." The girls laughed, and I broke down. I tried too hard not to make a sound.

"And the fact that she even thinks she's good-looking. Ha, she's not fooling anybody. Diana and Adelaide would be better off without her," the first girl said.

"It's funny because Diana said something similar to me before she went to Italy."

"I know—" the other one started but was thankfully interrupted when the door to the bathroom opened yet again.

"Aah!" one girl screamed.

"Get out, you pervert!" one said.

"Sorry, girls, but I have some business to do here, so I'm afraid I have to ask you to leave." Kai's voice boomed through the bathroom. It was his deep, sexy, and rough voice.

The girls scoffed and protested but left the bathroom, anyway. I was so shocked to hear that Kai was here, I started to hold my breath. Even the tears stopped falling.

"Astrid?" His voice changed tone. It was soft and worried now.

"Yeah?" I whispered just enough for him to hear. I was sitting on the floor now, leaning against the bathroom stall. It was very unhygienic, but I didn't care. Kai slid down next to me, a door separating us from each other's view.

"Want to get out of here?" he asked. I nodded, then I remembered he couldn't see me.

"Yes," I cried out. Before I could actually get up, his hand reached for mine, and he briefly intertwined our fingers. He squeezed before I let go, stood up, and opened the door. Slowly, his hands wrapped around me and pulled me into one of his gentle hugs where he held me like I would break at any moment. His chest was hard, but his heartbeat was soft and steady. Being around him made me feel safe right now. He made me feel better, but how could that be when even my own family couldn't?

He let me go and wiped one last tear from my cheek.

"Come on," he said, kissing my forehead and leading me out of the school. Nobody saw us leaving because, by the time we walked out, the bell had rung long ago and nobody was in sight.

Kai led me to his car—not motorcycle. I was grateful for this little detail because as much as it was exhilarating to ride on the motorcycle, I didn't feel up to it today.

As he drove, the words I heard people say kept replaying in my mind. I guess I was the girl who didn't have the guts to stand up for herself, and when she got hurt, she shut everybody out.

And then I thought about Kai.

His name echoed in my mind as I looked at him. The way his muscles moved, the way his mouth turned up when he smiled, the way he smirked when he wanted to say something sexually inappropriate—his whole bad boy facade fell apart that day he told me about his sister. What made him trust me enough to tell me? Was I worth it?

"You're staring." He pointed out.

I blushed and looked away.

"I love it when you blush." He confessed, making me blush even more. "Now you look as red as a tomato." He chuckled.

"Stop!" I winced. Kai smiled because he saw a small smile creep to my face.

"How you holding up?" he asked.

"I'm fine. Where are we going?" The curiosity got the better of me, and I finally remembered to ask.

"I need to show you something," he told me. Ten minutes later, he parked the car in a parking lot and turned to look at me.

"Do you remember when you dared me to try Oreos?" he asked, and I nodded, confused where he was going with this.

"Well, ever since that day, I became obsessed. So I surfed the internet a little and found an actual cafe that served Oreos, and I've been coming here ever since."

He actually loved Oreos that much? "Wow." I didn't know what else to say.

"Um…I've also been wanting to talk to you for a while, but you were so keen on ignoring me before, so I didn't get the chance yet. I know you are not ready for anything more than just friendship, and I respect that."

But did I still want that?

"Well, what do *you* want, Kai?" I asked him for the first time.

"Astrid…" He hesitated. "I've told you I liked you, but I never told you the truth. I've lied to you for a while now, and I'm sorry."

"What? Why?" I started to become paranoid.

"I…The first time I really started noticing you…It wasn't the accident or at school."

"What are you talking about?" I asked him.

"Did you go by the name Ella this summer?" he asked me.

"How do you know?"

"I spent the summer in California too. I used to go to the beach and surf. All of my friends knew you there as Ella. Luke was also one of my best friends, and he couldn't stop talking about you."

"Why don't I know about any of this?" I said to myself and gave Kai a very confused look.

"I recognized you as soon as you and Luke met at the bonfire. I don't know. I panicked and left, but I almost ran into you every single day."

"Why didn't you say anything?"

"I don't know!" Kai freaked out. "I guess…" He ran a hand through his hair in a way that clearly showed his frustration. "I wouldn't normally do this, but when I saw you there, something happened. It's like time stopped and all I could see was you. But if you looked at me, all you could see were the girls I had played with, drunk and half-naked. You would see all the alcohol and the party lifestyle. I didn't want you to see me this way. But you have to believe me. When I saw you, you changed my life, and you got into my head ever since then. The accident was just a coincidence."

"I…" I didn't know what to reply. Kai's gaze on me was intense, and we were still sitting in the car. He leaned closer, his hands resting on my cheek.

"I like you, Astrid, and I know you've made it clear you want to be just friends, but damn, I have to ask you at least this time when you're sober. Will you be my girlfriend?" There was silence for a moment while I looked at him. Instead of choosing the right words, I finally gave into the temptation.

I kissed Kai, and I didn't regret it.

Chapter 33

Kai took me to the cafe, and we sat down near the window. As soon as the waitress came to take our order, I requested hot cocoa with cream and Oreo cake. Kai got black coffee, strong.

He was far more relaxed now than I had ever seen him. It was like this secret was a burden to him. He distracted me from my life and my problems, and for that I was grateful. I sat next to him rather than across because he didn't want me too far away. He held my hand and occasionally kissed it or placed a kiss on my temple. He was gentle, and it was just what I needed.

I called my mom and told her the situation. She understood why I didn't want to be at school today, but when she offered to pick me up, I told her I was with Kai.

And for some reason, she wasn't surprised. I certainly was. My mom didn't ask any questions. She only told me to come home when I was ready.

"How are you feeling?" Kai asked on the drive home.

"I had my better days."

"Hadn't we all?" he said.

His hand squeezed mine before he grabbed the steering wheel. "Want to talk about it?" he asked.

I guess I would need to talk about it sooner or later, and I trusted Kai with so many of my burdens already.

"My grandpa…He was like another dad to me. Every summer morning, you'd see my dad and grandpa reading the newspaper as Mom makes them coffee. Around that time, Grandma would usually get home from the bookstore, bringing me books. We had a routine. My grandma and I annoyed Grandpa and Connor so much when we talked about books, exactly like how they annoyed us when they talked about sports." I smiled at the memory as my eyes started to water. "Grandpa was always the life of the party, encouraging us to play charades or board games. Nothing will be the same without him."

Kai's hand found mine yet again, and he held it tight. I was grateful for his support and thankful he was here. I knew we just became a thing, but the way he influenced my life was already the way I hoped to influence his.

"It sounds like he was a great man," Kai said in the end. I nodded and smiled, wiping away my tears as he parked his car in his driveway.

"Are you doing anything today?" he asked, and I could see he was nervous because his hands shook a little and his mouth twitched at his left side. It was really cute.

"Studying, catching up on homework. Nothing fun," I replied.

"Want to do something less fun?" he asked.

"Uh…no?" I said.

"Do you want," he started, trying to specify, "to help me with my biology?"

Then I remembered his problems with biology class.

"That hardly counts as less fun," I said.

"Is that a yes?" he asked. I nodded and leaned in to kiss him.

"Only if we do it in my room."

"Deal." He kissed me back.

We studied in my room until Kai couldn't focus anymore and tried to talk about other things. It was evident he hated biology.

"Come on, Kai. Biology isn't that boring." I tried to convince him, completely distracted from all my problems in life.

"Oh yeah? Tell me one good reason why." He raised an eyebrow. Immediately, I knew.

"Sex," I said. Kai gave me a look that was unreadable.

"Sex?"

"Yes. Sex. We're going to talk about it in a month or two."

"How do you know this?" Kai sneaked an arm around me. We were lying on the bed, side by side, with a book open in front of us.

"Because the teacher told us. Am I the only one paying attention in class?" I asked him. He nodded and smirked.

"Don't worry. I have a feeling we'll both be paying more attention in a month or two." I playfully hit his arm, and he gave me a look that only meant trouble. Before I knew what was happening, he started to tickle me, and soon, I was begging him to stop.

"Had enough?" he asked, and I nodded. He pushed me down so he was on top and kissed my jaw. Then his lips travelled to my earlobes. I exhaled softly, and when he pulled back, he smirked.

"It's nice to know I have an effect on you."

"You do not have an effect on me!" I denied even though it was hopeless.

"Really?" he asked, leaning down again. He kissed my lips this time—only so softly like the kiss was the brush of a feather. He teased me until I couldn't take it any longer. I was the one who pressed my lips to kiss him, and this one was definitely more firm and intense. He kissed me back, and I could feel his smile.

"Don't worry," he spoke, pulling away for a second. "You have the same effect on me."

He leaned down to plant another kiss on my lips as his hands travelled to my hair, and I felt the kiss deepen. It was the support I needed right now. I needed him to be here with me, to distract me, to make me feel safe in his arms.

And he was here. We got so lost in the kiss that when the door opened, we were startled.

"Hey, Astrid—"

At the threshold stood Matt with Connor, and they stared at us.

Uh, oh.

Chapter 34

Okay, Diary.

Let me break the situation down for you. Kai was on top of me. We were both lying on the bed, *and* we were kissing when my brother and Matt opened the door.

Was I in deep shit? A normal person would think that would be the case, but what surprised me was that things turned out to had a different way of resolving themselves.

In fact, it was Connor who spoke first.

"Oh, my eyes!" he started screaming. "Cover yourselves, both of you!" he yelled at me, obviously joking though I had no idea how he got into such a good mood.

"Connor, stop being an idiot." I scolded him with a very serious voice. He looked back at us and raised an eyebrow at Kai.

"Are you going to get off my sister or what, Asher?" Connor asked Kai. Kai only smirked and hugged me tighter.

"Nah, I think I'm good." Kai wanted to give me another kiss, but first, I was too embarrassed to kiss him in front of my brother and second, I saw Matt's look, and it was pained. I gently pushed Kai off me and sat up.

"Okay, I think you've had enough," I said to my boyfriend, making him pout. And let me tell you, it was the cutest pout ever. I turned to Connor who was still waiting for me.

"What do you want?" I sighed, feeling slightly embarrassed to be caught. I wasn't used to having a boyfriend and acting all lovey-dovey in general. Especially not when my brother was around.

"Matt and I are going to the Winterheart bookstore. I wanted to ask you if you want to come, but I see you're busy." Connor winked. Wait, was he serious? Did my overprotective brother give me a 'go ahead' sign when it came to Kai? I was caught speechless because I did not understand his thinking in any way.

"*Or* you could both cancel your love making and come with us. You know, judging from how excited you seemed the last time you were there."

I looked over to Kai who was smirking. "Sure," he said before I could reply, and I think I just figured out Connor's plan. This was all a distraction. He knew that Kai and I were together now—everyone did since that party.

Getting up, I dismissed Matt and Connor so I could get ready, all the while hearing their protests because Kai was still in my room. "That's because he's my boyfriend!" I yelled. Suddenly, a pair of arms wrapped around my waist, and he leaned down and whispered.

"You've got that right." He kissed my earlobe as I turned around and gave him a brief kiss on his cheek before heading to the bathroom.

When I came out, Kai was stretched out on my bed like he owned it. Of course, only he would think that.

"Come on," I said, waving him to follow me as I grabbed my wallet. Kai took my hand, and we rushed outside where Matt and Connor were already waiting in the car. Of course, the guys wanted to separate us, and I ended up driving. I loved doing it so much. My brother, on the other hand, hated to drive with me.

"Come on, Grandma. Speed it up," Connor said, nagging.

"You know what, Connor? I'm driving faster than your brain works, so shut up," I snapped.

"At least my brain works," Connor said.

"At least I have a brain," I replied to him, and he stuck his tongue out at me. "Real mature," I muttered. At the back, I heard Matt say to Kai, "Imagine being stuck with them in the car for hours."

"What was that, Matilda?" I asked, getting slightly annoyed.

"Nothing." He flashed a smile, not really offended by my nickname for him.

"Sure," I said.

"Hey, Astrid. Where are you going?" Connor said, and that's when I really concentrated on the road.

"Oh, crap!" I said. I forgot to turn right.

"Nice job, Einstein," Matt said.

"Shut up." I shot at him and sighed. "Well, boys. Looks like we'll be driving for another twenty minutes."

We accidentally got on a highway, and there wasn't any way for us to get off anytime soon.

I was stuck with them for the whole ride, but at least Kai didn't say anything. Finally, we arrived at the bookstore. Kai and I immediately bolted right after I threw the car keys at my brother.

Kai followed me to the young adult section. There was as much real excitement in his eyes as I was sure was in mine.

"Have you read this one yet?" Kai asked. He was talking about *These Broken Stars*.

"Not yet, but I heard a booktuber talk about it."

"A what?" he asked. I noted that he looked cute when he was confused.

"A booktuber, someone who uploads book related videos on YouTube, a bookworm who likes to read and talk about books in their videos."

Kai looked so fascinated with this new information, I couldn't help but smile. "You never heard of booktubers? Sasha Alsberg for example?"

She was my favourite. Sasha Alsberg was not only funny and amazing, but she was also extremely down to earth, sweet, and humble.

Kai shook his head and asked, "What are you, then?"

"I'm a bookworm and a book reviewer," I said.

"We need to spend more time together so you can teach me all of this nerd talk I can't seem to understand."

I rolled my eyes in amusement as we checked out all the books available. "Do you want a good book to read?" he asked.

"Sure," I said.

"*Sweet Evil.*"

"What?" I asked.

"*Sweet Evil* by Wendy Higgins. It's a sweet book full of evil. Get it? No, but seriously, I just started reading it, and it's pretty cool," he told me and pointed where the book was placed on the shelf.

After reading the blurb, I decided I wanted to get it. Kai and I looked around for a bit, and we realized that Connor and Matt were spying on us for some reason, so Kai got an idea and show them something they didn't want to see. He led me to the section for eighteen plus books like *Fifty Shades of Grey* and anything by Sylvia Day.

I picked one up, but Kai showed me a completely different book.

"Want to buy two copies of this and read it together?" he said, standing closer to me.

"You mean like a book club?" I asked, sounding like a complete and total nerd. Kai only shrugged and said, "Sure, why not?"

I agreed, and then he leaned down for a kiss only to get interrupted.

"You are not reading erotic books together even if I have to drag you away from him myself!" Connor said rather loudly, his chest puffed out to look more intimidating.

That made Kai and I crack up. See, Kai knew how overprotective he was from spending time around Connor. And while dating his sister, he knew that he had to act decent so he could be around me. However, that still didn't mean he couldn't mess with him.

When I thought about it, I actually thought it would be a good idea to read a more mature book together with Kai. I guess that would be a great experiment, and it made me smile just thinking about it...If he could keep his hands off me, that is.

"Connor, if you don't get out of my face in ten seconds, I swear we will start reading this book together just to annoy you," I said to him. It took Connor five seconds to move, but by then, he was already pushing it.

"I'll drop by tomorrow and get us two copies," Kai whispered as my brother and his annoying best friend left to wait for us by the door. I laughed under my breath as I shook my head and headed to pay for *Sweet Evil*. Usually, I picked up lots of books when I was in the bookstore, but for some reason, I didn't today.

Or so I thought until I saw a few more books that interested me. The woman told me how much I had to pay, and just as I was about to pull out my credit card, Kai said he would pay and handed the money to the cashier.

I looked at him, stunned by his actions. Did he just pay for my books? Kai gave me one of his dazzling smiles.

"I read your blog post. I know that paying for your books is the number one thing you desire in a boyfriend. Besides that he must like to read."

I would have jumped him right there because what he said was just so damn attractive to me. What he did was so damn overwhelming.

"You did your research," I said, trying to keep myself from sounding impressed, but I failed.

"Only for you, love," he said and leaned down to give me a kiss.

It was starting to get dark by now, and when we got to the car, Connor was already in the driver's seat, and Matt was in the passenger's.

"Finally, they're giving us some freedom," Kai said with a wink. I blushed. I somehow could not get used to him flirting with me.

"I know," I said as we sat in the car, and my brother drove us home.

Chapter 35

Dear Diary,

A week had passed, and within that time, there was a funeral, my grandma moved in, my parents temporarily moved out, and a crap load of tests.

Sighing, I threw myself onto my bed, exhaustion coursing through my body. I wasn't just physically tired, but there was also mental weariness. It had been a complete chaos, organizing the funeral while making sure my grades were up. Never in my entire life did I wish to read and disappear more than I did now.

But somehow, I wasn't able to. I was lying in my comfortable, cosy bed, freshly changed into my pyjamas and hoping to get some sleep. However, as soon as my eyes started to close, I heard a sound next door. Not a noise, it was more like very, very loud singing.

I groaned as I forced myself to sit up and look to Kai's side. Oh my God. He was only in his boxers. I flushed in embarrassment and felt a slight violation of privacy. I did not want to see him almost naked, and I was sure he didn't want to see me spying on him. Well, actually, I wasn't so sure about the latter.

I avoided his gaze, not really sure if he noticed me or not, but I went to pick up my phone and plug it into my charger. The battery was almost dead.

I called his number. It didn't ring two times before he answered.

"Hey, princess."

"Kai, do me a favour, will you?" I said to him.

"Anything for you."

"Next time you decide to run around your room singing half-naked, please close the curtains and keep your voice down. I'm sure nobody wants to be that mentally scarred for life," I said to him, and he laughed.

"Oh, come on, I'm your boyfriend. Besides, I'm sure you've seen a guy naked before," he spoke, and I stayed quiet.

"You haven't?" he asked like he couldn't believe it. "Hold on one sec." He hung up the phone. It didn't take him three minutes to climb into my room.

"Kai!" I hissed. I knew my grandma was downstairs in the guest room while Connor was in the room across from mine. He could probably hear us talking.

Kai casually shuffled to the door and turned the key to lock it. He was used to doing this by now because we didn't want anyone disturbing us while we were spending some time alone.

Not that we were doing anything. It was just that we usually talked about all sorts of private things. I really got to know him better because of it.

He sat down beside me on the bed. "You've never seen a guy naked?" he asked. "Then how did you have sex?" Kai raised an eyebrow.

"Who said I had sex?" I hissed. Kai gave me the think-about-it look, and when I did, I wanted to kill him. Of course! Connor and his friends!

"Who thinks I already had sex?" I asked him.

"Everyone at school," he informed me. "Rumours spread fast, especially if Matt starts them."

"Wait, what?" Matt started it? Not that it was true, but why would Matt want people to know?

"Yeah, wait. So you didn't have sex?"

I shook my head. "No," I said to Kai. "Nor do I want to until I'm sure I'm ready."

"Then why would the guys think…"

"Connor and his annoying friends wanted to give me the sex talk, and I said I didn't need it. It somehow made them think I already did the deed. I didn't deny nor confirm it because it was none of their business in the first place."

"So you made your brother think you've already had sex? How furious was he on a scale of one to ten?" Kai smirked.

"About an eight. So far, it was the angriest I've ever seen him."

"You have no idea how angry he was when he told the guys in the locker room." Kai was laughing now.

"What the hell are you guys talking about in the locker room?" I remembered the bet that one of my best friends mentioned some time ago before the big football game.

"Nothing." Kai suddenly became serious.

"Uh-huh," I said, clearly not believing him, but as much as I was curious, I didn't want to push it, so I kept my mouth shut and minded my own business.

"Why didn't you tell me before you didn't have sex yet?" Kai asked, sneaking an arm around me and making me lie beneath him on the bed.

"I assumed you knew," I said, which wasn't a lie.

"Well, I'm glad I know now. It just means I'll have to be more considerate and give you more time."

"You're already being considerate." I brushed a strand of hair out of his face.

"I want it to be something special. I want you to remember it." He kissed the top of my nose.

"I'm sure I'll remember it, alright."

"I just hope you'll feel safe around me. I hope you'll trust me enough to give me the honour of being your first. That's all."

I was touched by how thoughtful he was. Kai was really something special. He started playing with my dyed blonde hair, and I liked it.

"I already trust you. You make me feel safe. I'm just not ready yet."

"I know, and I'll wait for as long as you want."

With that, he gave me a goodbye kiss and disappeared into his room.

Some time later, I was finally able to fall asleep in my soft bed.

Chapter 36

Dear Diary,

A week ago was Diana's birthday. She was hosting a party tonight, so Addie and I had been invited as co-hosts to make sure everything was perfect. As much I wanted to, I knew I couldn't say no to her. If I went to other parties and wore silly dresses, would one more night kill me?

Besides, it was Di, and I could never refuse her. Well, almost never. Kai was also invited, but we weren't going together. Addie and I had to be there sooner to help Diana prepare. Her party was usually one of the biggest parties of the school year. Yes, my best friend threw awesome parties people talked about forever.

When I arrived at Diana's house, it was almost six PM. I didn't go to her party when Vanessa died and the year after that, so this was my first time after it happened. Although I might have not been there, I knew everything that was going on because like I said, people talked about Diana's parties for a long time.

Was I nervous today? No.

Oh, who was I kidding? Maybe then. I didn't know how to help Addie with what she had in mind and Diana with her luxurious birthday wishes. Something told me she didn't actually want me to do anything but just wanted me to be there. And that was one thought that comforted me as I rang the doorbell to the huge mansion that was Diana's house.

Her maid opened it and let me in. Having been there lots of times, I walked in the direction of Di's room, my gift in hand.

I drew Lily Collins and framed it for her. I also bought an autograph of Lily Collins on eBay, which I hoped would make her happy.

Before I could even knock on the door, the birthday girl swung it open and dragged me in.

"There you are! Are you excited? I know I am. Oh God, but I'm also nervous. What if Beck comes? You need to help me get ready! I can't look like this!" Diana started to ramble like always, so I took her by the shoulders and squeezed, willing her to calm down. She took a deep breath, but I knew she was excited to have me here.

"This party's going to be one of the best parties of your life. You're going to enjoy it no matter who's here and how you look. Got it?" I said. Diana nodded. "Now tell me, why do you want to know if Beck's here?"

I remembered when Kai told me he saw Diana and Beck kissing, but I always forgot to ask about that. I just assumed they were too drunk to remember.

"I don't know!" She leaned her head and hugged me, letting out a frustrated sigh. I glanced over to Addie who just shrugged.

"Okay then," I said. "We might as well head to work."

In the end, Diana looked like the most graceful queen. Her dress was a red ball gown that made her look mature. Then, we made sure the house was perfect. Before we knew it, it was ten minutes until ten, and nobody was there yet. Everybody knew not to show up too early.

Diana had Addie and I stay in the room with her until she was ready to come out.

"Girls," she said, raising a glass of champagne she said her parents gave her for her seventeenth birthday. They said it was a special occasion, and Diana apparently took it without any objections.

"To an awesome year and to my eighteenth birthday." We both cheered and drank up. That was all I was going to drink tonight.

By eleven PM, the party was up and running mostly in the backyard that was almost as huge as the whole house. There was a swimming pool that people seemed to enjoy. Cups were lying everywhere, and I just got a headache when I thought about us cleaning it up in the morning.

"Hey." I felt arms wrapping around me. I turned around to see Kai. I felt myself smiling, and he pulled me in for a kiss.

As much as I enjoyed his kisses, I never got used to the idea of us dating and making it public. It felt so weird that *the* Bad Boy was not much of a bad boy after all. He was just trying to keep his reputation up so nobody would ask about his family or pry into his personal life.

It looked like others weren't that used to it either because they gave us strange looks. Some girls even gave me looks of hostility.

"Hello to you too." I smiled at Kai before Diana called me over to her side, waving frantically.

"Uh-oh. Queen emergency." I gave Kai an apologetic look, and he nodded, making me promise to be right back.

As soon as I neared my best friend, she grabbed my wrists and pulled me closer so she could whisper in my ear.

"He's here. He's here!" she hissed. "What do I do? What do I say?" she asked, panicking.

I glanced in the direction she was looking and saw my brother and his friends, but I had a feeling Diana was staring at Beck. What the hell was going on between the two? Wait, was she asking me for advice? She was the queen of parties, the queen of flirting, not me. Well, not usually.

"Act normal," I ordered. She nodded way too nervously, and I gave her a look that made her calm down. The guys headed over in our direction.

"Talk to me," I said to Diana. "Where's Addie?" Diana was a great actress, but I could still read from the way she was standing that she felt anxious.

"Addie is with Reese," she said, pretending we were having that conversation.

"Of course. I have a feeling the two of them will disappear before the party's over." Diana shrugged, and we both smiled. The couple even started saying 'I love you' to each other. I had no idea when Kai and I would be ready to take that step. I was going to leave that to him.

Before Diana could reply, the guys appeared beside me.

"Happy late birthday," Beck said, kissing Diana on the cheek. I had a feeling her cheeks were getting warm, so I distracted the guys by asking them what they thought of the party, and I got a grateful look from her.

"It's amazing," Nathaniel replied.

"Almost." Connor and Matt agreed.

"What do you mean almost?" Diana almost sounded angry. No, wait. She did sound angry because we have all spent hours preparing for this party and days planning it.

"Relax. We're kidding." Connor smiled. He and Diana never got along because they teased each other a lot, but it seemed that Connor was in a good mood today.

"You're such a pig," my best friend told my brother as he stuck out his tongue at her, making me smile.

I quickly glanced over at Kai and noticed that he was talking to a girl with the shortest dress ever. A flash of jealousy and anger went through me.

"Trouble in paradise?" Matt whispered, enjoying this way too much.

I gave him a mean look and glanced back, worried Kai would do something stupid. But as soon as the girl tried to touch his arm, he moved away and said goodbye.

"Nope," I replied to Matt right after Kai met my gaze, and we smiled at each other. Matt looked almost furious when I turned my attention to him, but that didn't matter. I was glad that Kai decided to stay away from that girl.

"Excuse me," I said to the guys and headed over to where I saw Delilah standing.

"Hey there, Delilah," I said, and Delilah hugged me.

"Hey, Astrid." She glanced around. "Awesome party. You drinking?" she asked me.

"No," I replied seriously.

"Neither am I," she said, surprising me. Delilah was usually the first girl drunk. Well, not comatose but drunk.

"Are you pregnant?" I raised an eyebrow.

"What? No!" she said. "I just…Diana is my friend, and I want to enjoy this night hanging out with friends and actually remember it."

We talked a little and then said our goodbyes afterwards. After that, Hunter Riley, one of Kai's friends, came over and tried to talk me up and flirt with me. I tried to stay friendly, but when I wouldn't respond, he sighed.

"You really are hard to get, aren't you?" he said. As soon as he said that, Kai appeared by my side.

"Yes, and she's mine," Kai growled. "Back off." Hunter put his hands up in defeat but winked at me. In a way, I liked Hunter because he was funny. He was really cool too, and I got all that from my five-minute conversation with him.

"Well, well, well. Aren't we possessive?" I asked and smirked at Kai who didn't think this was funny in any way.

"You are mine. Mine," he said in a dead serious voice. "Don't forget that." His eyes were intense, but so was the next kiss he gave me that spiralled into one that was full of hunger.

When I pulled back, he gave me a puzzled look.

"Same goes for you." I was talking about the girl from before.

Having said that, I turned around and walked away.

Chapter 37

Dear Diary,

Time passed, and without me even realizing, it was the middle of February. Kai slept over a lot. We had movie marathons, and Matt still tried to get to me, paying no attention to Kai's overprotective warnings. Whenever Matt was around, I felt nervous. *He* made me nervous and uncomfortable. Somehow, though he was always hostile like before, he tried to flirt with me.

My brother even said to him once that he should leave me alone. It didn't work. Matt was stubborn, and I had a feeling something was going on.

That tension between us always made me want to run from my room.

One relatively warm day in February, I realized how much more confident I felt than a couple of months ago. I even started to consider going on Broadway after high school—like what Mom tried to convince me over the past few years. I started to attract more attention online as well. Instagram Celebrities often gave me a shout out our two.

Speaking of Mom, she was currently at work while my dad was still out of town. I saw them only a couple of times over the past few months. They'd been too busy with everything—always travelling back and forth whenever a potential buyer appeared.

While I was updating my blog, my phone started ringing. Opening the text message, I saw Connor's number pop up on the screen. He wanted me to come downstairs to say hello to his company. I immediately texted back no as a response.

A few short moments later, there was a knock on my door, and I sighed, knowing very well it was my brother. He invited himself in and plopped down on my bed, making himself completely at home.

"Hey, Sis," he spoke first. "How's life?"

"What do you need, Connor?" I closed my laptop and placed my hands on my knees.

"The boys want you downstairs," he said to me.

"So?" I replied in a resigned voice. He should have known by now.

"Why are you avoiding us?"

"I'm not. I just don't like your company, and you know that very well."

"Why? Is this because of Matt? Something's going on, and you can't hide it from me, Astrid. I'm going to find out sooner or later, so we might as well get on with it."

"Nothing's going on." I denied. "You know how he's treating me, and you don't do anything about it."

"Because you seem to have grown a thick protective skin over the last few months. So excuse me if I think you don't need my help."

"He wouldn't leave me alone ever since Kai and I announced that we were a couple. It's not my fault I don't like him, and he should just realize that."

"Stop being such a drama queen," Connor said in exasperation. "He doesn't care about you."

"He doesn't?"

"No. He's just angry that he lost a bet. That's all," he said to me, not watching his words.

"A bet? What bet?" I sat up straight and rushed to the door before Connor could escape. I had never seen my brother try to bolt so quickly, and now that he was trapped, he started to panic.

He scratched the back of his neck and suddenly turned very, incredibly pale. "It doesn't matter?" Connor spoke to me, but it seemed more like a question.

"What are you hiding from me?" I questioned him.

"It's nothing, really."

"Connor, Goddamn it, answer the question!" Snapping seemed to be the only thing that helped. "What bet? What does all of this have to do with me?"

Deep down, I already knew what he hid from me. It would have made sense—the way people at school treated me, all their laughs behind my back, all their whispered comments of how naïve I was. Normally, I dismissed it as something that had to do with Kai.

Finally, Connor gave up and sat down on my bed again, his eyes looking at anything but me.

"There was a bet made some time ago," he started. And a memory came to mind—Diana and Addie talking about it in my room. "We were all in the locker room talking about how you became such a..."

"Loser?" I asked, my knees starting to shake.

"I wasn't going to say that." Connor looked away.

"It's not like I'm hearing it for the first time from you, Connor. Now tell me what happened."

"Matt started talking about your friendship with Vanessa which was a weird topic, but the guys seemed to hear it for the first time."

That's how Kai knew me as the girl who lost her best friend. He wrote that in his letter.

"So one thing led to another, and Matt started bragging on how he thought you had a crush on him because you'd always stutter when he was around. Mason countered that it was probably because he insulted you so much that you figured it was better to be quiet. The two got into an argument. One thing led to another, and they made a bet."

"What was the bet about?" I asked, but I knew. I knew, I knew, and I knew.

"Mason said that Matt can't get you into his bed by the time you get a boyfriend. Which seemed easy to him because Matt thought you'd never get a boyfriend, so the bet was already his."

"What?" I looked at Connor with so much rage, so much surprise, and a lot of hurt.

Was this all just a game to him? And to Matt? For a moment, I thought they actually cared about my feelings, and now that I thought back to all the moments with them, all the moments at school, my heart kept breaking.

Connor rushed to explain, but I was only half-listening. "I didn't warn you because the guys said that anyone who'd try would be kicked off the team one way or another. They all love a good bet. I was positive you'd refuse him. I know you, Astrid. You push people away."

"So that made it okay for you to not tell me?" I raised my voice, but it broke in the middle of the sentence. I wouldn't cry at them. They were bullies, always. "I can't believe you. I had your back no matter what, and the first opportunity you have, you stick a knife into mine. We are twins. You were supposed to tell me!"

"Astrid, please," Connor pleaded.

"No, you know what? I'm done. If you think you can play me—Oh my God! Is Kai a part of the plan?" The shock of the news was spreading, but I paid no attention to it.

"Astrid, come on," Connor said, stalling.

"Tell me. Did he know about the bet?"

Connor stayed silent, and his silence told me more than his words could have.

"And what about everyone at school? Is that why people were laughing at me and mocking me this entire time? Is that why everybody treats me like I'm stupid?"

He was silent once more until he spoke up. "Diana and Adelaide also knew," my brother finally confessed.

"Classic," I said, and that did it. I opened my door and left the house. I took the keys of my grandma's car and drove until there was only darkness left on the street.

I stopped driving when I realized where I was going. The graveyard was a creepy place at night, but the numbness masked the terror and made it almost welcoming. I didn't care about anything but her. I was seeing her for the first time after the funeral.

When I reached the grave, her name was written on the tombstone, and just seeing that made me collapse and cry.

"I tried to be strong, Vanessa" was the first thing I spoke. "I tried to move on. I tried to surround myself with people I love, but those people...All your life you fear the monsters under your bed when it's the humans you should be wary of." Only silence welcomed my rambling.

"I miss California. I miss being away from this place. It was the only time I felt like I could piece myself back together. Maybe it's because people there didn't keep shattering me piece by piece."

I looked down and took a deep breath, trying to contain my tears. "If I stay here, I know I won't be happy. I may pretend, but that's all it is. It's like pouring alcohol on a fire raging in your soul. You stay, but you're not living. And I know you'd want me to go. You said so yourself, but I'm afraid of the unknown. What if this is what all my life will be? What if this is as good as it gets?"

Thunder answered my question, and I looked up. "I'm being a drama queen, I know. It's what everyone keeps telling me."

I smiled a bit and then straightened my posture. "I guess I really don't have a choice, do I? It's either stay here and be stuck in my bubble or go out into the world and make something of myself."

I stood up, finally coming to a decision. "Thank you, Vanessa. This won't be my last visit." I promised her as I wiped my tears away. "I miss you."

I stared at her grave for a few moments before turning around and getting into my grandma's car. The road was slippery, and the storm started raging, but I managed to get to the hospital safely. I ran inside to hide from the rain as I searched for my mom.

I came up to the front desk and saw the familiar face of Nurse Tasha. She was one of my mom's best friends.

"Are you okay?" she asked, seeing the current state I was in. To be honest, I would have been worried too if I saw the way I looked.

"I'm not physically hurt," I told her. "But I need to see my mom."

"Your mom is currently on a lunch break, but I can call her if you want," Tasha asked, and I nodded.

She came three minutes later, and it shocked me to see her in nurse uniform even though that was her job. The moment my mother saw me, her strict face fell, and worry flashed in her eyes.

One of the doctors was her friend, and he let us use his office while he saw a couple of patients. My mother thanked him before leading me inside.

"What's happened, honey?"

"Remember when you said you wanted me to move to New York and go to a boarding school?" I asked her.

She nodded. "Has something happened?"

"I want to give that a try," I said to her without really answering her question. "You're not there for me when I need you," I spoke, not really accusing her but stating a fact. "You never saw me come home and cry after some stranger from school humiliated me in front of everybody. You never knew about people cutting up my clothes while I was in PE or putting sticky notes on my back. Those notes, Mom, they said some horrible things. You never heard me get insulted. You didn't have to wash brand new clothes after some girl spilled some juice on you because she thought you deserved it. You never knew about the bullying, nor did you know that Connor and his friends picked on me the most. You didn't know how badly I've been treated, and that's not your fault. It's mine."

It was the first time I saw my mom break down. I told her about everything. I told her about the day Grandpa died and the notes I'd been getting in my locker. I told her about the time some girl pushed me in front of a moving car, and I almost got hit.

"I don't belong here, Mom. I'm different from these people, and I was too afraid to admit it because I thought it was a bad thing. But you know what? It's not. I do not have to take any of this, and sometimes, being quiet and leaving is better than staying and picking a fight with everybody. I want to find my place in this world where I don't have to be someone I'm not."

I just wanted to be Astrid. Just Astrid. No insults, nothing.

"Do you want me to go in there and say I'm not feeling well? We could maybe get something to eat and talk," my mom asked. I knew it was selfish because there were people who needed her more than I did, sick people inside the hospital.

We ended up at a café I never visited before, and I was still shaking from shock.

"Honey, calm down," my mom tried to soothe me, but it didn't work.

"I just wish for once that I could start over. I just don't want to be surrounded by all this," I told her.

"Do you really want to leave your life here?" I took a deep breath and nodded. "Okay then. I'll talk to your father."

And that was what happened. She called Dad and booked my flight to New York. I came home briefly to pack my stuff while Mom sent Connor to pick up Grandma. She helped, and we were done within half an hour before I was at an airport.

Seeing the planes, I tried not to have a panic attack as everything inside of me was shaking. I felt sick to the stomach, but I wasn't alone.

My mother squeezed my hand in support as she sent me off on a new adventure. Though my anxiety and fear of planes almost got the best of me, I took a deep breath, and for the first time, I knew this was where I was meant to be.

I wish I could write more, describe more, but this is the last page. I'll buy a new diary when I get to New York—if I make it there alive. Sorry, I wouldn't be me if I hadn't written that.

Signed: Astrid Ella Bailey

Can't get enough of Astrid and Kai? Make sure you sign up for the author's blog to find out more about them!

Get these two bonus chapters and more freebies when you sign up at *desirae-clark.awesomeauthors.org*!

Here is a sample from another story you may enjoy:

LEIGH FRANKIE

AFTER SCHOOL
WITH
MR. OBNOXIOUS

Prologue

"Hey, Aaron, you imbecile creature!"

Aaron Lanter stopped dead in his tracks as soon as he heard his name and the derogatory word that came after it. He did not like it. He was Aaron Lanter, the most popular guy in school, every girl's dream guy and every guy's object of jealousy. He was the Aaron of Lediville High. Who on earth would call his attention by calling him an imbecile?

The culprit was none other than Samantha Banks, who stood proudly by the countertop with her rather worried friends in the kitchen.

"What did you just call me?" Aaron asked. The party was beginning to bore him. He and his friend, Zack, decided to leave the party when they passed by the kitchen.

"Imbecile," Sam answered coolly. "Hey, spell imbecile, I-M-B-E-C-I-L-E."

"You're screwed, Sam, like down the sewer kind of screwed," a girl who looked like a gothic doll said.

Sam frowned at her friend. "That doesn't even make any sense, does it? Oh, I feel warm fuzzies."

Chloe was nodding her head between Sam and the gothic girl to the rap music blasting loudly. "This is an amazing party."

She has never been drunk in her entire existence. But in that gusty Friday night, she let her best friend, Chloe, influence her decision on how she should spend her evening. If it were up to her, she would be curling up in bed, watching classic TV show reruns. In fact, it was what she had planned, but when Diana, one of Lediville's cheerleaders, announced a house party before the first period even started Monday morning, everything changed.

For days, Chloe wouldn't let the topic rest; she begged Sam to go with her, promised her they would leave the party before midnight. And on Thursday, Sam finally gave in and agreed to go with her. Chloe victoriously manipulated Sam to join in on the fun with half of the population of Lediville High.

After a few arguments about the smell of alcohol in the entire house, Sam finally agreed to stay for four hours. It was the first party of the school year, and everyone was partying like it was their last. The place was already swamped, but surprisingly, the kitchen wasn't, so they decided to hang out in there with two other girls from one of their morning classes.

It only took three bottles of beer to turn Sam as pink as salmon and a bit deaf. She started to laugh and talk louder than normal. When boredom slowly crept in, the girl with the shiniest red hair they called Ginger suggested that they play Truth or Dare.

"Yes. Let's play that 'cause this party sucks," another drunk girl agreed. She had her nose pierced and couldn't seem to stop playing with her pierced tongue. Her eyes were locked on a guy and a girl pinned to a wall, making out.

Chloe rolled her eyes. "Just because nobody wants to make out with you doesn't mean the party sucks, Martha."

The girl who got both her nose and tongue pierced frowned. "Who'd want to make out with jerks?" She started to stare at the two girls standing in front of them surrounded by four guys.

The redhead suddenly stood up and almost spilled her beer all over Sam. "Okay, let's entertain ourselves and play Truth or Dare," she suggested again.

"This is Diana's house. She's a popular cheerleader. Why don't we look around and maybe we'd find some weird stuff? Wouldn't it be fun to discover something about one of those perfect cheerleaders at our school?" the goth girl said.

Martha shook her head. "You have issues you need to fix, Luna," she said.

Sam got up. "Chloe, I think we should go. I'm starting to feel weird. I can't feel my hands."

Chloe checked her watch. "Sam, it is quarter to ten. We agreed to leave fifteen minutes before eleven." She offered Sam another bottle of beer while the other three had additional bottles too. After a couple more beers, Ginger proposed again that they play Truth or Dare.

And they all finally went for it. When it was Sam's turn, she didn't even hesitate to choose dare.

Dare. Samantha Banks chose dare, a choice she made which she would regret making for the rest of her senior year because as soon as Ginger saw Aaron and his other jock friend pass by, she was doomed.

Kiss Aaron Lanter, on the lips, with your tongue, for ten seconds— was the dare.

Chloe, Ginger, and the gothic girl froze as Aaron walked to them.

"Oh, Sam, did you really have to call him imbecile?" Chloe muttered. She was growing nervous as few teens from the crowd started to gather around, waiting for what was about to happen.

"Who are you?" Aaron asked Sam. He looked really pissed.

Sam, on the other hand, was drunk and didn't really care what was going on. "My name is Samantha Banks, your majesty, a humble servant from nowhere land." She further ridiculed Aaron with a curtsy. "Actually, I know you know me because we had four classes together last school year. But you just pretend you don't have a clue since you're the so-called heartthrob, and you're brainlessly following this preposterous social structure where a socially well-accepted person such as yourself would and should only acknowledge other popular peoples' existence. And since I am obviously neither cool nor popular, hence the 'Who are you?'"

"Excuse me?" Aaron said.

"Is she drunk or high?" the gothic girl whispered.

"Let's go, Sam. I think we drank more than enough booze for tonight," Chloe said. She had more than five bottles; however, Sam's alcohol tolerance was low compared to hers.

Sam had already turned red, not because of the tension everyone in the kitchen started to feel, but rather due to the effect of the fourth bottle she had. She walked over to Aaron, smiling. "Listen, my friends and I are playing Truth or Dare. I chose dare. Now, I have to kiss you."

Some giggled, and some just stood there with *uh-oh* looks on their faces.

"Is she serious?"

"Where's Nicole? She's got to see this?"

"What did you just tell me?" Aaron couldn't believe what he was hearing.

"Whoa, dude. Nerdy got hots for you. Respect!" Zack, Aaron's jock friend, mocked.

"Oh, please." Sam rolled her eyes. "Like you've never kissed before? It's simple. My tongue plays with your tongue and then we swap spit. Like this."

And before Aaron could even express his displeasure, Samantha Banks, Lediville High's nobody, grabbed his collar and slammed her mouth against his before everyone's eyes.

"What the freak?" Gothic Girl covered her mouth in shock.

"Could this really be happening?" Chloe thought she might faint.

"Is it the end of the world already?"

"The Illuminati is real after all."

Sam could not care less about the over the top comments from the stunned spectators because, much to her surprise, Aaron's mouth opened as soon as their lips touched. Her tongue forcefully whirled around his mouth. And the second she felt the heat inside Aaron's mouth and took in the sweet smell of his breath, her head started to slowly spin that she had to wrap her arms around him for support.

"Way to go, Sam!" Ginger teased.

"Shit! Nicole's coming."

As soon as Chloe heard someone from the crowd mention Aaron's girlfriend, she knew she had to do something. "Okay, that's enough lip-locking." She yanked her friend away, abruptly ending a semi-perfect example and display of how nerd girls could turn wacko when drunk. "We seriously have to go."

"I think I'm gonna throw up." Sam moaned.

Aaron looked down at her, speechless and in total disbelief just like the rest of the people who witnessed the shocking highlight of the party.

"What's going on here?" It was Nicole.

"Shit. Nothing. We're outta here." Chloe hurriedly grabbed Sam, dragging her out of the house and saving her from Nicole's wrath.

Music was still blasting from the living room, and others were still busy in their own world, but in the kitchen, the atmosphere was utterly different. No one said a word.

If you enjoyed this sample, then look for
After School with Mr. Obnoxious.

Introducing the Characters Magazine App

Download the app to get the free issues of interviews from famous fiction characters and find your next favorite book!

iTunes: bit.ly/CharactersApple
Google Play: bit.ly/CharactersAndroid

Acknowledgements

First, I'd like to thank the wonderful team from Blvnp Publishing, my agent, all the editors, and everyone who worked so hard on this book. You are all such a vital part to publishing it, and I am so blessed to have worked with such a wonderful team.

Mentioning Jeacqlina Kreich is a must. She's been there when times were rough and knew how to make me smile. Without her, I'd be completely lost. And then my other friends from school—you've always been good at letting me know that writing was something I was good at, and you've had no problem being happy for me whenever something major happened. You were also extremely good at telling me I talk about books too much.

It's impossible for me not to thank Sasha Alsberg (her personality, her videos, her obsession with Scotland and Sam Heughan, her success and her hard work made her who she is today and she deserves recognition, and I'd still like to imagine that one day, we'll become friends who talk and meet for coffee to discuss our latest book obsessions), Sarah J. Maas, Lindsay Cummings, Rick Riordan, Cassandra Clare, Diana Gabaldon, Wendy Higgins, Jennifer L. Armentrout, Becca Fitzpatrick, and all other amazing authors that impacted my way of writing the way they did.

Thanks to my Wattpad friends (Em, Aashi, Claudia, Ellie, Elle, Hasnita, Harsh, Nicola, Noelle, Locky, Ellison, Alayna, Sami, Millie, Miranda, and all others I might be forgetting) and the whole Wattpad team. You have made writing a lot more fun because we did it together.

I'd also like to mention my Youtube family—Dino, Severin, Anita, Alex, and Laura. You have inspired me to be creative in more ways than I ever thought was possible. Thanks also to my international friends—Courtney, Lili, Caoimhe, Pranati, Nicole, Qing, and Yara.

My family has been crucial to my writing. My sister—she had to listen to me talk about my ideas for hours and never complained one bit. My dad—the patient, loving guy who would do anything to make his daughter the happiest girl in the world. Then there's my brother—the guy with a unique character who sometimes inspired more difficult scenes to write. Kristina, the girl who always knew the right things to do and the right things to say. My grandma who fed me during my writing sessions, my uncle and my grandpa who made sure I was warm enough, and my other relatives who have in some way or another impacted my life.

Lastly, I'd like to thank everybody who made my life harder. I'd like to thank the people who have mistreated me, insulted me, put me down or laughed behind my back. You are the ones that in the end made me stronger. You are the ones who made Astrid who she is. You have enabled me to write a relatable character, one many of my readers could see themselves in. You are the ones that now have to see how much your bad energy motivated me and brought me to where I am today.

Author's Note

Hey there!

Thank you so much for reading *My Bad Boy Neighbor*! I can't express how grateful I am for reading something that was once just a thought inside my head.

I'd love to hear from you! Please feel free to email me at desirae_clark@awesomeauthors.org and sign up at desirae-clark.awesomeauthors.org for freebies!

One last thing: I'd love to hear your thoughts on the book. Please leave a review on Amazon or Goodreads because I just love reading your comments and getting to know YOU!

Whether that review is good or bad, I'd still love to hear it!

Can't wait to hear from you!
Desirae Clark

About the Author

Desirae Clark is a student from Slovenia. When not spending time on Wattpad, she likes to daydream about books and fictional characters.

Her favorite activities are writing, book buying and reading—though book hangovers are her "best friends" and constant companions. She is absolutely in love with Scotland and would wish to study there in the future.

Like her on Facebook: http://bit.ly/Desirae-Clark

Follow her on Goodreads: http://bit.ly/DesiraeClarkGR

Sign up on her blog for freebies: http://bit.ly/DesiraeClarkWeb

CPSIA information can be obtained
at www.ICGtesting.com
Printed in the USA
FSHW010720070719
59767FS